DC SuperHero Girls™

The HERO in YOU!

My AMAZING Adventure Journal

_____

(YOUR NAME)

Published in the United States by Random House Children's Books, a division of Penguin Random House LLC, 1745 Broadway, New York, NY 10019, and in Canada by Penguin Random House Canada Limited, Toronto. Originally published as *DC Super Hero Girls Scribble Book* by Puffin Books, an imprint of Penguin Random House Ltd., London, in 2017.
Random House and the colophon are registered trademarks of Penguin Random House LLC.

randomhousekids.com
dcsuperherogirls.com
dckids.com

Written by Lauren Holowaty

ISBN 978-1-5247-1845-9 (hc)
Printed in the United States of America
10 9 8 7 6 5 4 3 2 1

DC SuperHero Girls™

The HERO in YOU!

~ My AMAZING Adventure Journal ~

Random House 🏠 New York

WELCOME TO SUPER HERO HIGH!

Always wanted to be a super hero? Eager to find out what goes on inside the walls of Super Hero High School? Well, you're in the right place. This activity journal is all about getting creative, meeting other SHHS students, unleashing your powers, and, most importantly, being your super self.

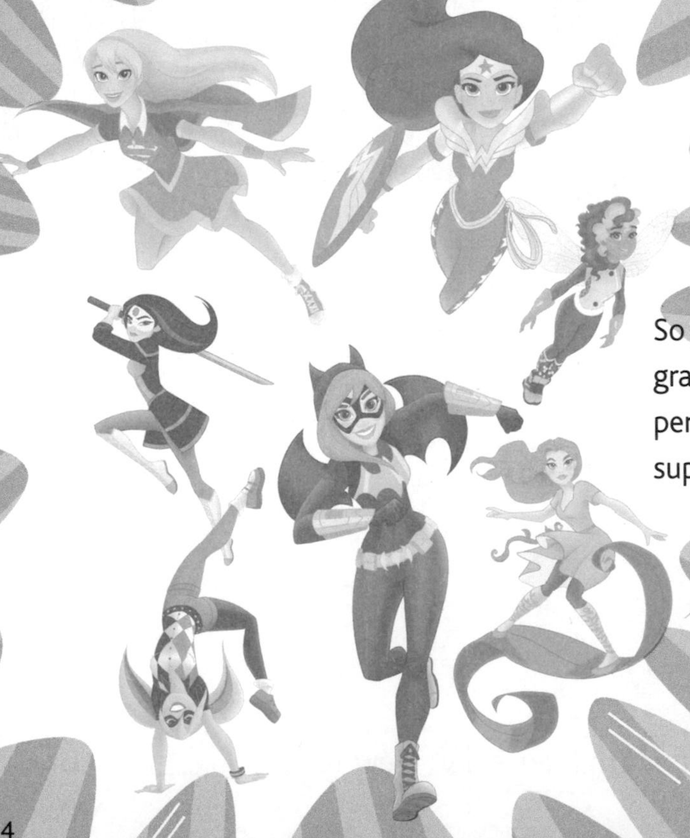

So get your cape on, grab your pens and pencils, and start your super hero training!

ABOUT ME

Name: Isabella Marai Mashni

Age: 11

Interests: super girl,

Why I want to be a super hero:

WHAT'S YOUR SUPERPOWER?

Answer the questions below, then turn the page to find out which superpower suits you the best.

1 Your idea of a fun weekend is . . .

a. Doing as many sports as you possibly can
b. Reading about fascinating new inventions and discoveries
c. Racing around doing as much as superhumanly possible
d. Going to a party and practicing your new dance routine

2 Friends are for . . .

a. Supporting you through hard times
b. Debating with
c. Racing against
d. Clowning around with

3 You're late for school, so you . . .

a. Pick up the school bus and carry it to get there faster
b. Quickly come up with a clever shortcut
c. That's impossible — you're never late
d. Leap and cartwheel there as fast as you can

4 Your favorite class is . . .

a. Phys Ed
b. Math
c. Any class with a timed quiz
d. Dance

5 Your favorite food is . . .

a. Anything with a strong flavor
b. Fish — it's great brain food
c. Fast food
d. Anything that'll boost your energy even more!

6 You would describe your dress sense as . . .

a. Bold
b. Smart
c. Streamlined
d. Quirky

7 Someone's standing in your way. You . . .

a. Carefully lift them out of the way
b. Cleverly explain why it makes sense for them to move
c. Find a fast way to get around them
d. Somersault over them

8 You would describe yourself as . . .

a. Independent and determined
b. Smart and eager to learn
c. Quick and agile
d. Energetic and flexible

9 You would prefer to spend your pocket money on . . .

a. Weights
b. Clever gadgets
c. Cool new running shoes
d. Gymnastics classes

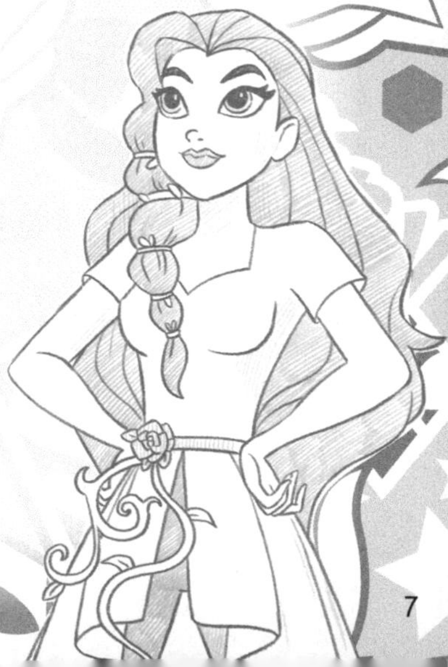

WHAT'S YOUR SUPERPOWER?

QUIZ RESULTS

Add up how many of each letter you circled on the previous pages, then read below to discover which superpower suits you best.

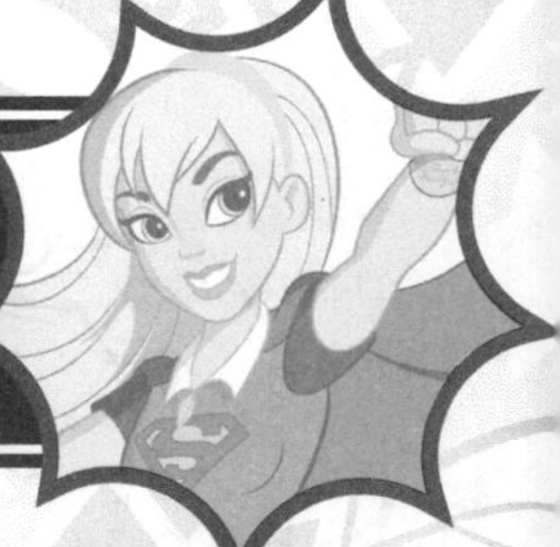

IF YOU CHOSE MOSTLY "A," THEN SUPER-STRENGTH WOULD BE THE PERFECT SUPERPOWER FOR YOU.

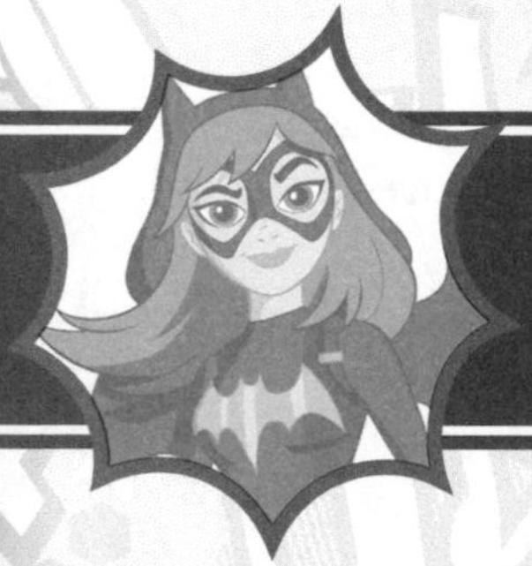

IF YOU CHOSE MOSTLY "B," THEN YOU PROBABLY ALREADY HAVE AWESOME BRAINPOWER.

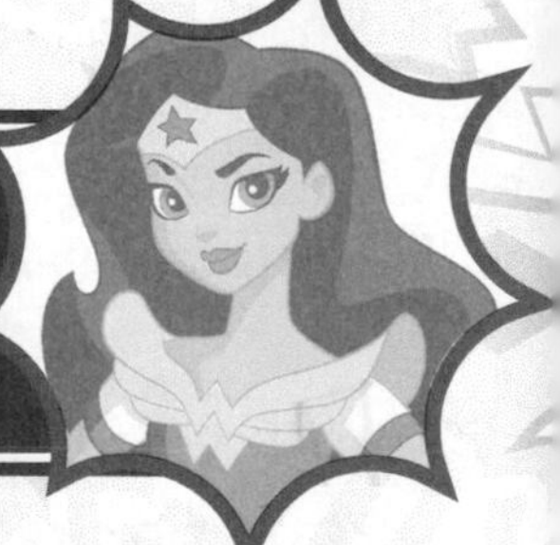

IF YOU CHOSE MOSTLY "C," THEN YOU NEED SUPER-SPEED!

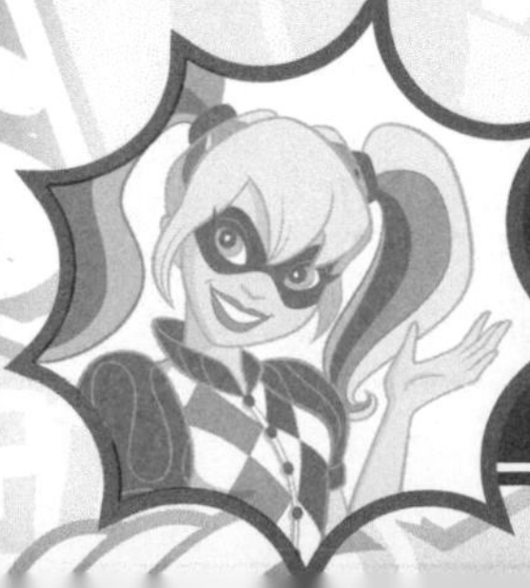

IF YOU CHOSE MOSTLY "D," THEN AMAZING ACROBATIC POWERS WOULD SUIT YOU.

MY SUPER HERO NAME

Choose one word from each column below to help you find your super hero name, or just make up your own name from scratch!

Write your super hero name on the line below.

Ultra	Girl
Brain	Woman
Mega	Fire
Shadow	Cat
Lightning	Teen
Poison	Bee
Atomic	Star
Power	Ivy
Beast	Claw
Iron	Hawk

Lightning Girl

MY SUPER HERO STYLE

Design and label your own super hero outfit and accessories. Make sure your costume is practical for racing around and fighting crime in!

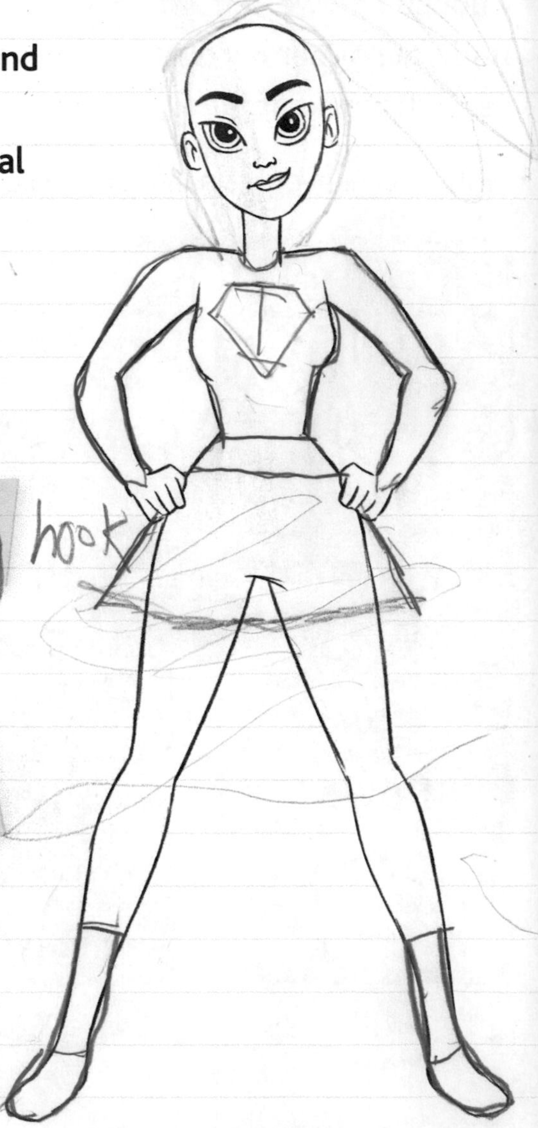

grabling hook

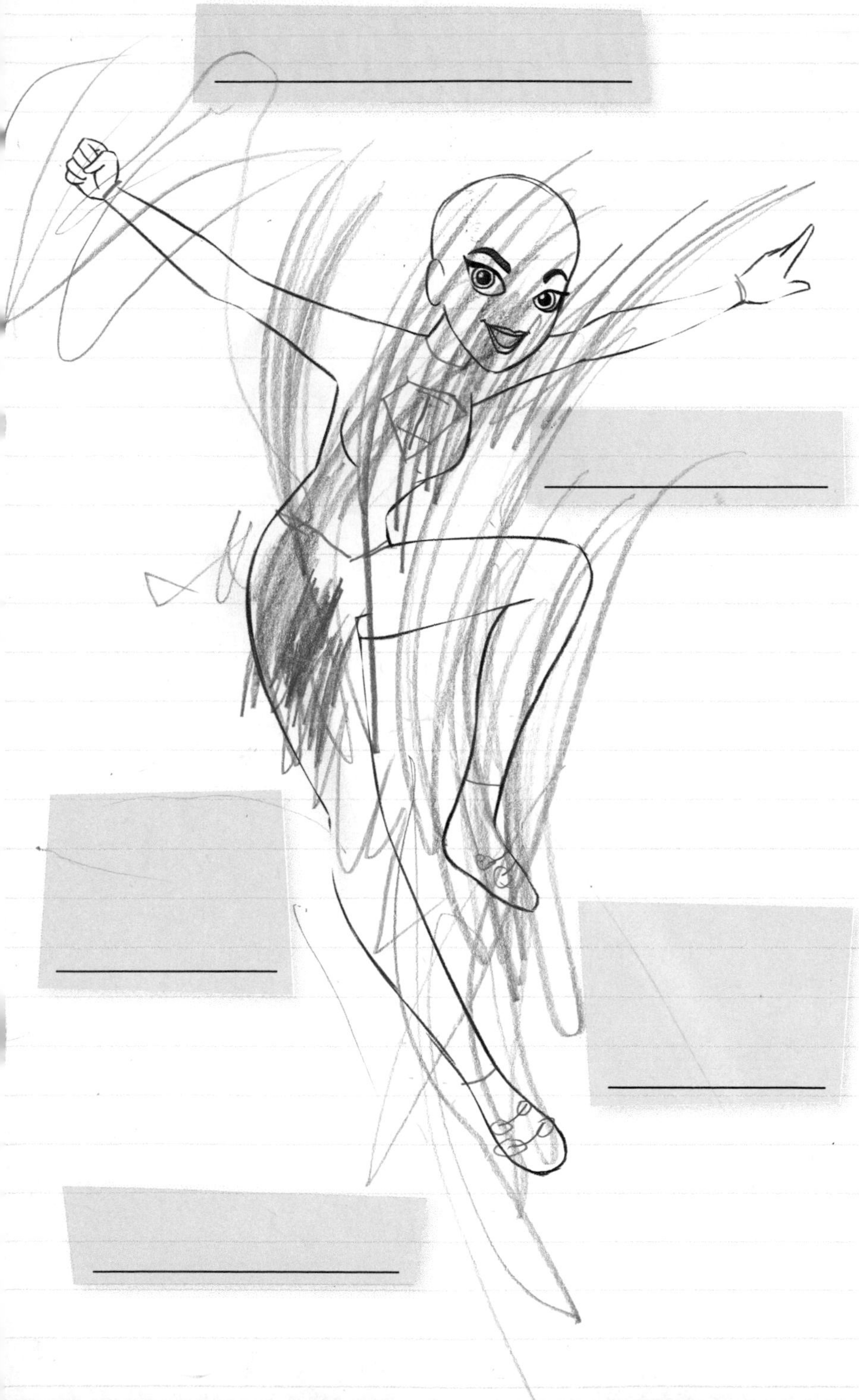

MY SUPER HERO SYMBOL

Wonder Woman has an awesome symbol!

TM

Create your own symbol for your super hero identity here.

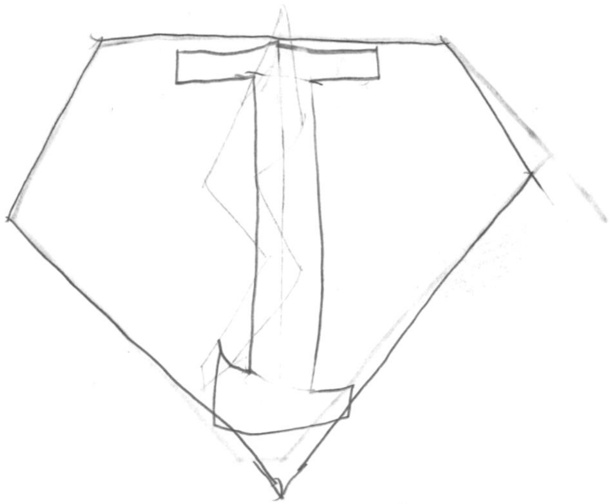

SUPERPOWER TOP 10

What top 10 things would you do with your superpower?

1. help people
2. fight crime
3. help Build
4. stop car chase
5. put bad guse in Jail
6.
7.
8.
9.
10.

UNLEASH YOUR POWERS!

Choose superpowers, super gadgets, or amazing abilities to deal with each situation on the next page. Take inspiration from the DC Super Hero Girls' powers and gadgets!

THE DC SUPER HERO GIRLS' POWERS AND GADGETS:

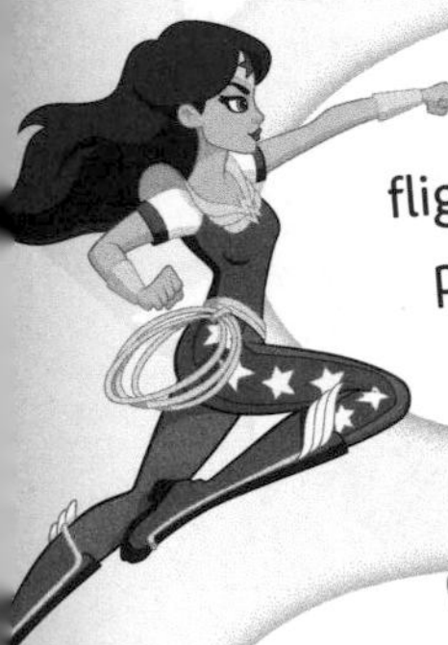

Wonder Woman: flight, Lasso of Truth, extra powerful shield, bullet-deflecting bracelets

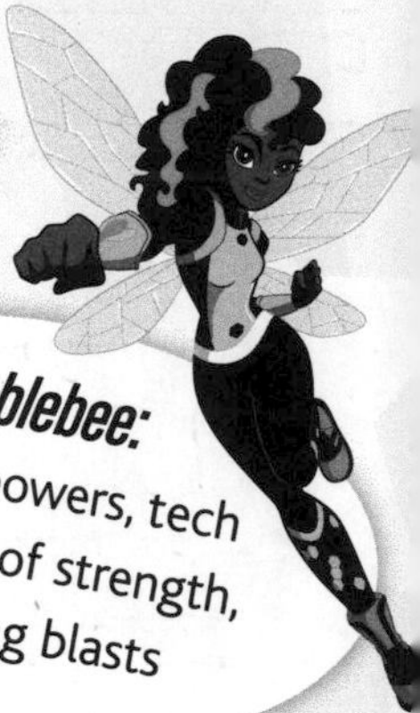

Bumblebee: shrinking powers, tech genius, suit of strength, sonic sting blasts

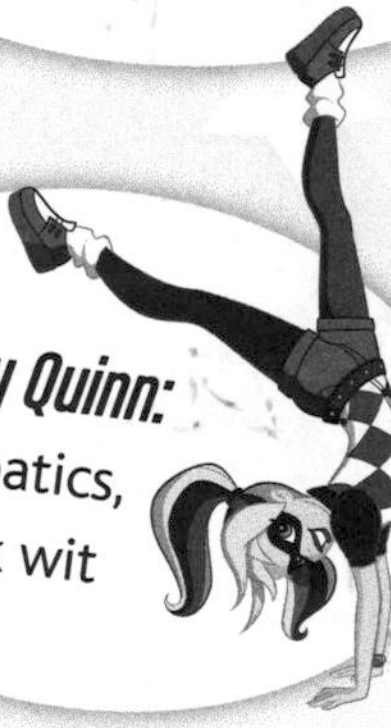

Harley Quinn: acrobatics, quick wit

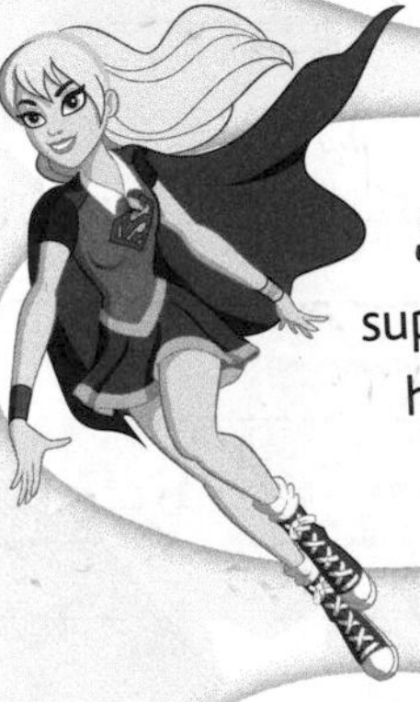

Supergirl: super-strength, heat vision, positivity

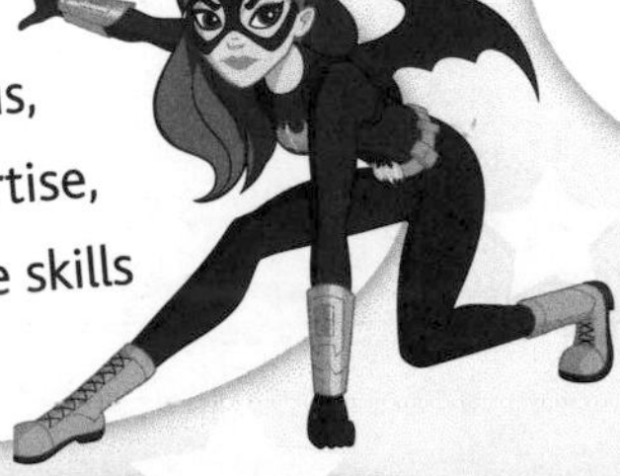

Batgirl: computer genius, martial-arts expertise, advanced detective skills

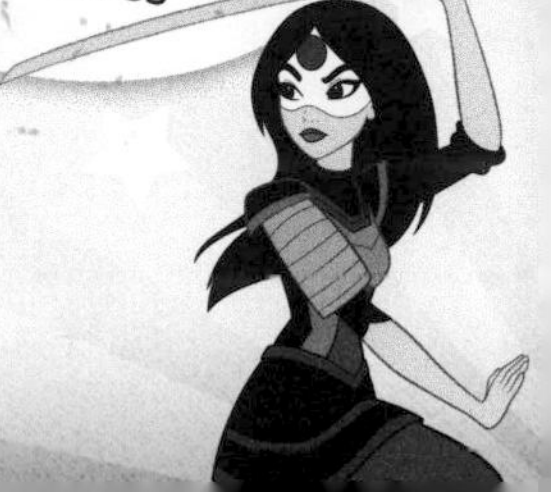

Katana: samurai sword skills, martial-arts expertise, fearlessness

SITUATIONS

1 You're in an extremely tight situation — four heavy stone walls are closing in around you, and there's only a tiny space above to escape! What do you do?

I would use super-
strength to move the
rocks.

2 A sneaky cheat has been taking everyone's super hero homework books and copying from them. What do you do?

I would use the
computer and se
how was stealing the
books

3 A mystery super-villain has hacked into Super Hero High School's computer system. What do you do?

I would try to
find the villain and
fix the computer syst-
em.

4 Metropolis has been brought to a standstill by a terrible ice storm. Everything is frozen! What do you do?

I would use heat
vision to melt the
ice and snow

TRUE IDENTITY

Every super hero is unique. Doodle over these schoolbooks to show your truly individual super hero self.

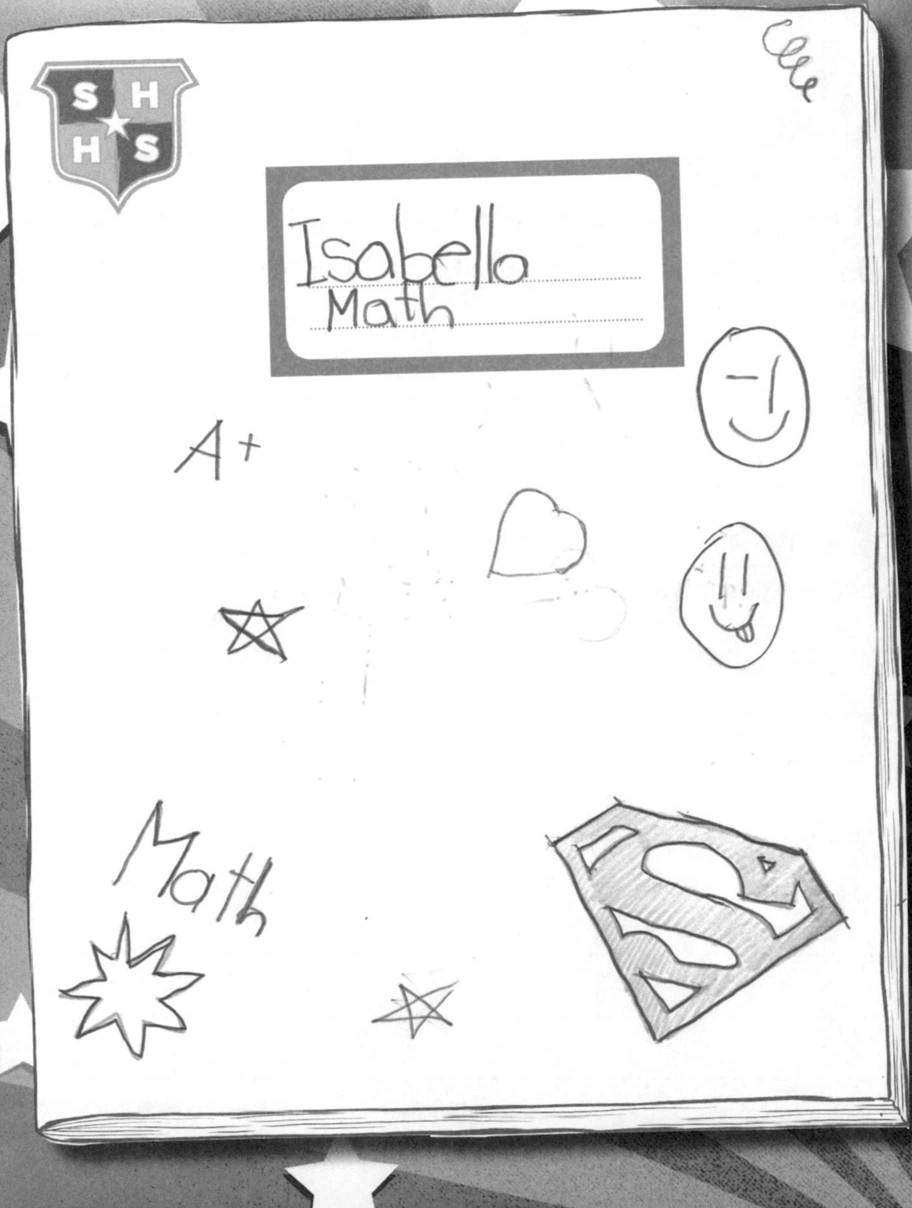
S H H S
Isabello
Math
A+
Math

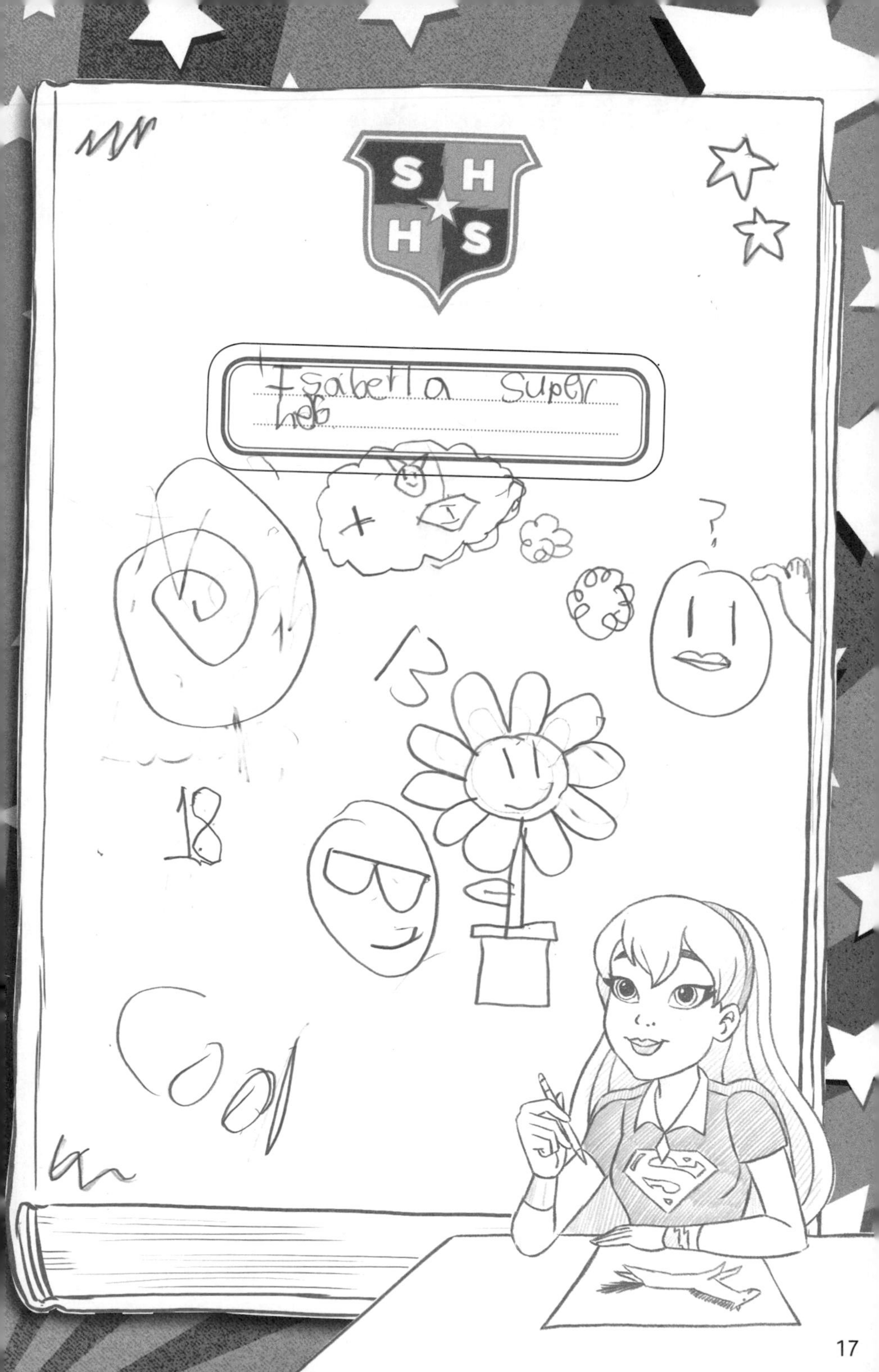
S H
H S

Dorm Room Designs

Design and decorate your room at Super Hero High School with your own super style.

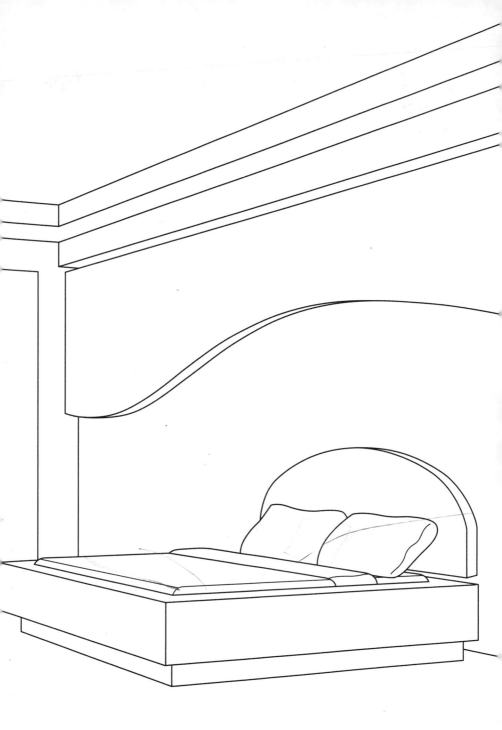

19

MY SUPER HERO FRIENDS

Pack these pages with your favorite pictures of you and all your super hero friends. Remember to include captions explaining how you just saved the world!

SCHOOL SCHEDULE

Complete a timetable full of your dream subjects —
all suitably superpowered, of course!

MONDAY	TUESDAY	WEDNESDAY

THURSDAY	FRIDAY

SUPER HERO MANEUVERS

Every super hero needs to think and act fast. Circle the speedy maneuver you would pull in each situation. Be as fast as you can — there's no time to lose!

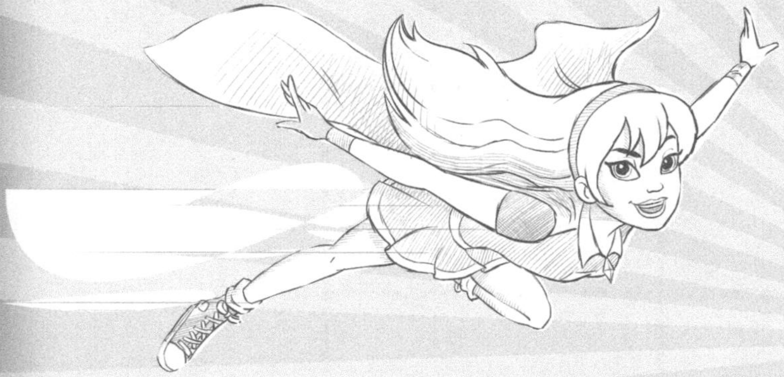

1 You're on a rescue mission and you're stuck in a traffic jam. To get around it, you . . .

A. **Jump** B. **Fly** C. **Slide** D. **Somersault**

2 There's an asteroid heading toward you at seriously high speed. You . . .

A. **Duck** B. **Leap** C. **Run** D. **Catch**

3 You've just been pranked in front of a crowd of people. You . . .

A. **Bow** B. **Hide** C. **Run** D. **Fly**

4 You're on board a ship and it's sinking fast! You . . .

A. **Swim** B. **Dive** C. **Float** D. **Bail**

5 A super-villain jumps out in front of you. You . . .

A. **Fight** B. **Fly**

C. **Defend** D. **Jump**

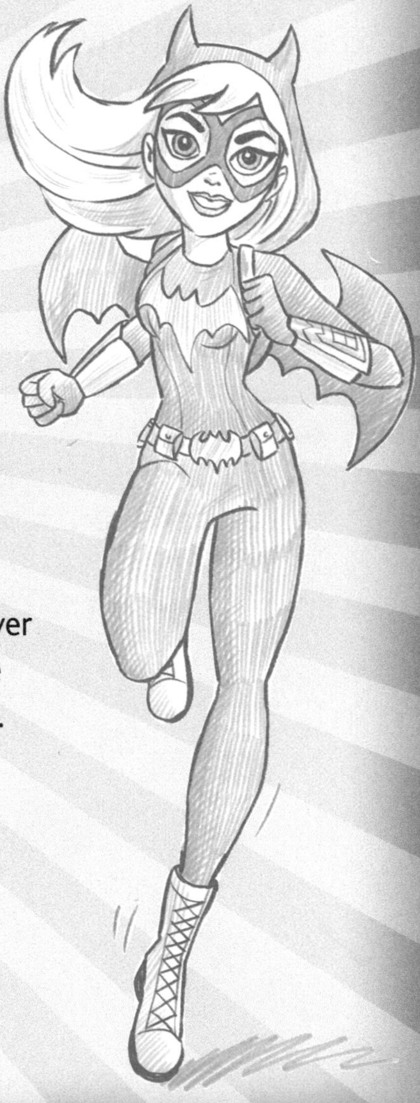

6 You arrive at a party and discover you're accidentally wearing the same outfit as your BFF. You . . .

A. **Change** B. **Run**

C. **Laugh** D. **Dance**

POWER JEWELRY

Not only do Wonder Woman's bracelets look really cool, but they deflect bullets and lasers, too. They're the perfect defense against super-villains! Design your own powerful accessories that look awesome and help you to fight crime.

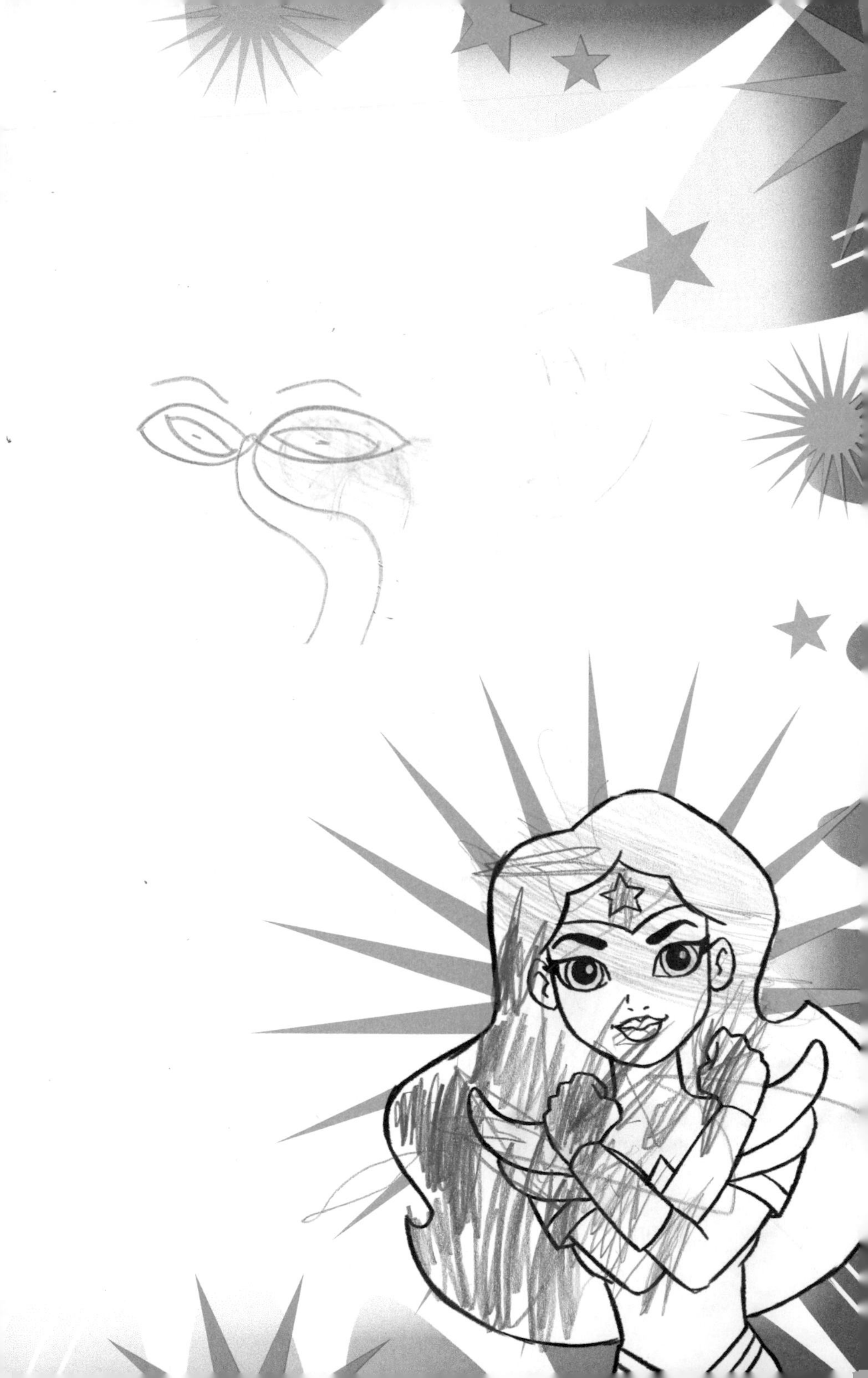

AFTER-SCHOOL ACTIVITIES

How would you like to spend your superpowered spare time? Check off the hobbies and clubs you would try out.

 Metropolis Junior Detective Society

○ The United Planets Club

○ The Band Club
(Join us if you feel the beat in your feet . . . or tentacles, or paws, or whatever.)

○ Science Club

○ Anti-Evil Engineering Society

○ Knitting and Hitting Club

○ Improv Drama Society

✓ The Yearbook Team

✓ Gardening

Quick Assignment:

HAWKGIRL NEEDS HELP!

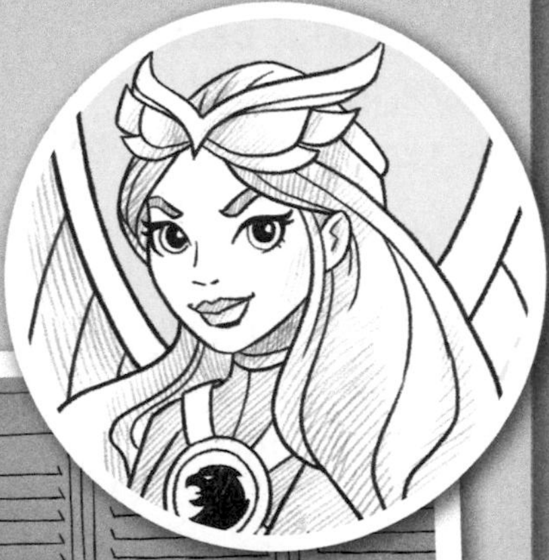

Hawkgirl is trying to work out who decorated the lockers as a prank. Use your observation skills to deduce which student did it. Circle her picture.

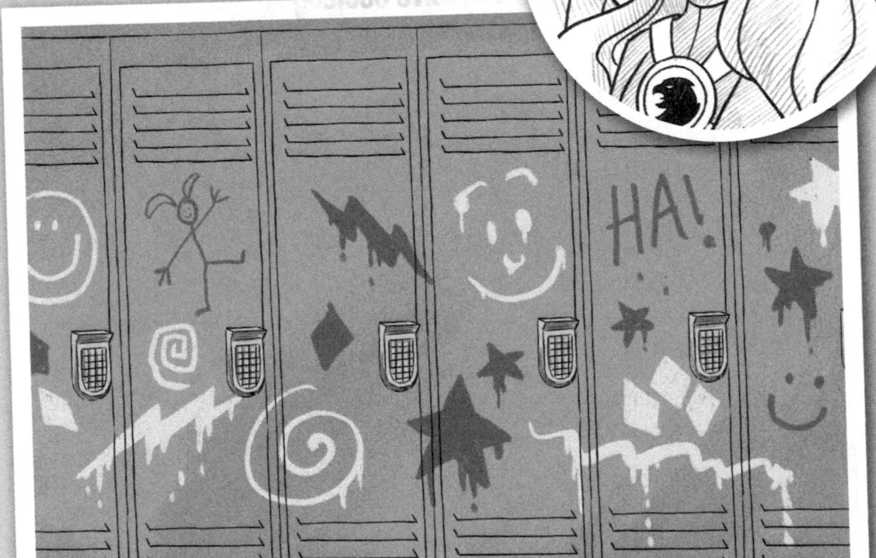
HA!

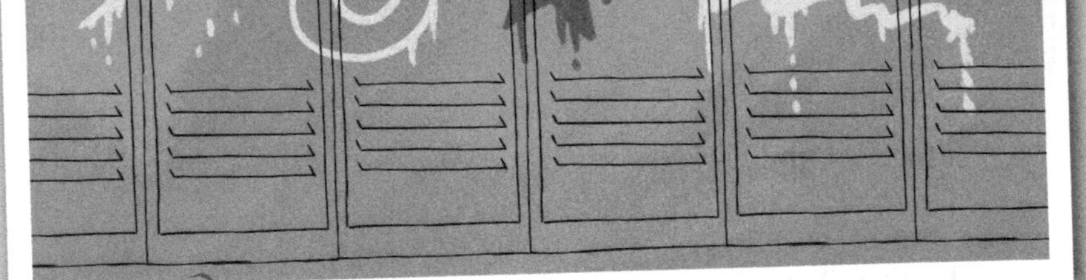

Answer: Looks like Harley Quinn's the culprit!

What Makes You You?

Write a list of words that best describe you. Then use them to draw a portrait of yourself, like this one of Harley Quinn!

MISCHIEF MAKER
MISS CLOWN
CLASS CLOWN
ACROBAT
HARLEY QUINN
OVER THE TOP
PRANKSTER
FUNNY
AGILE
SUPER
SWEET
JOKER
HERO
HA HA
HE HE

THE ART OF BEING SUPER

The girls have a cool new art project—they're making a mosaic! Add tiles of your own design to fill these two pages.

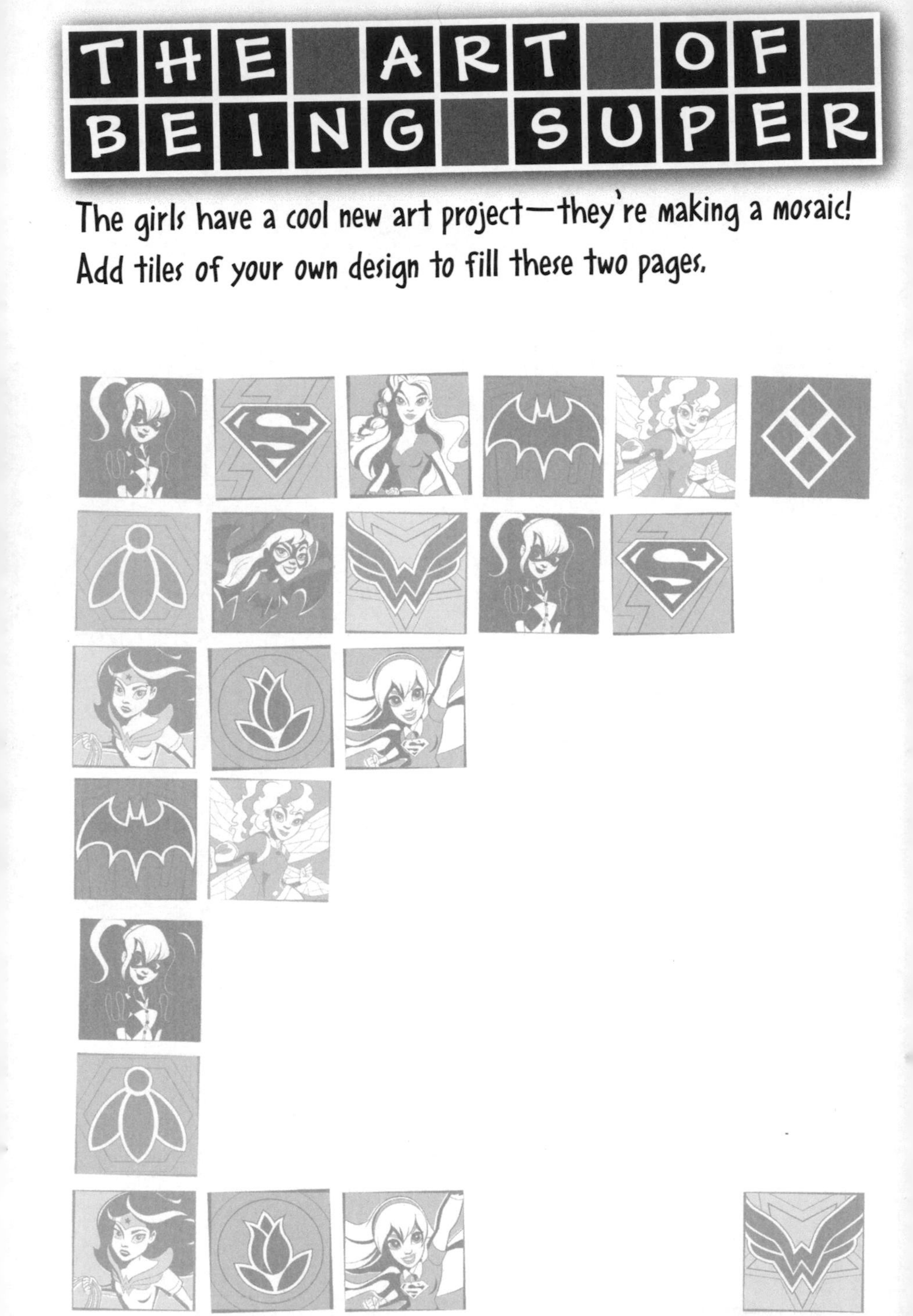

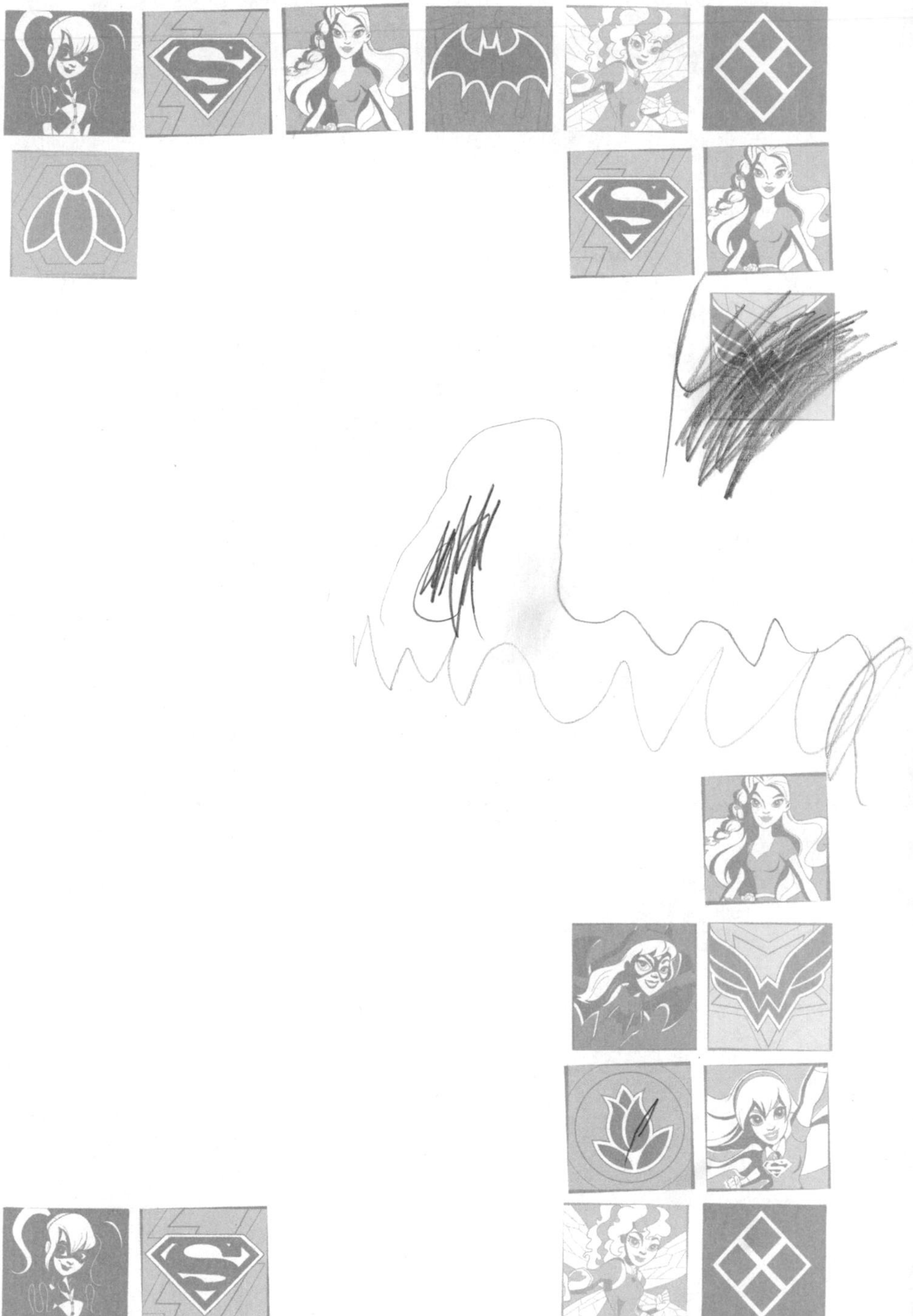

Join the Class

Meet some of your Super Hero High School classmates! Color them all. Then choose a study buddy.

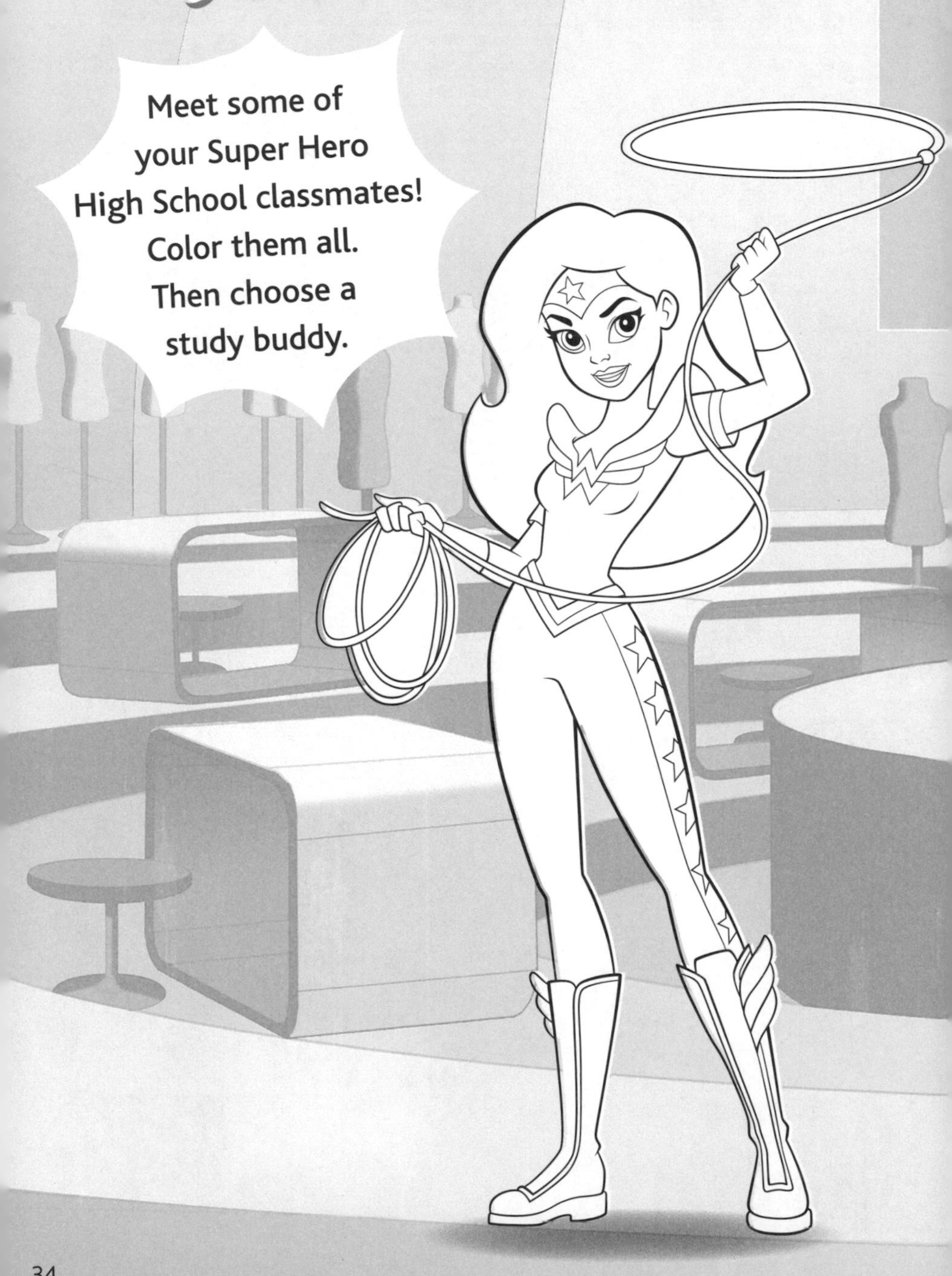

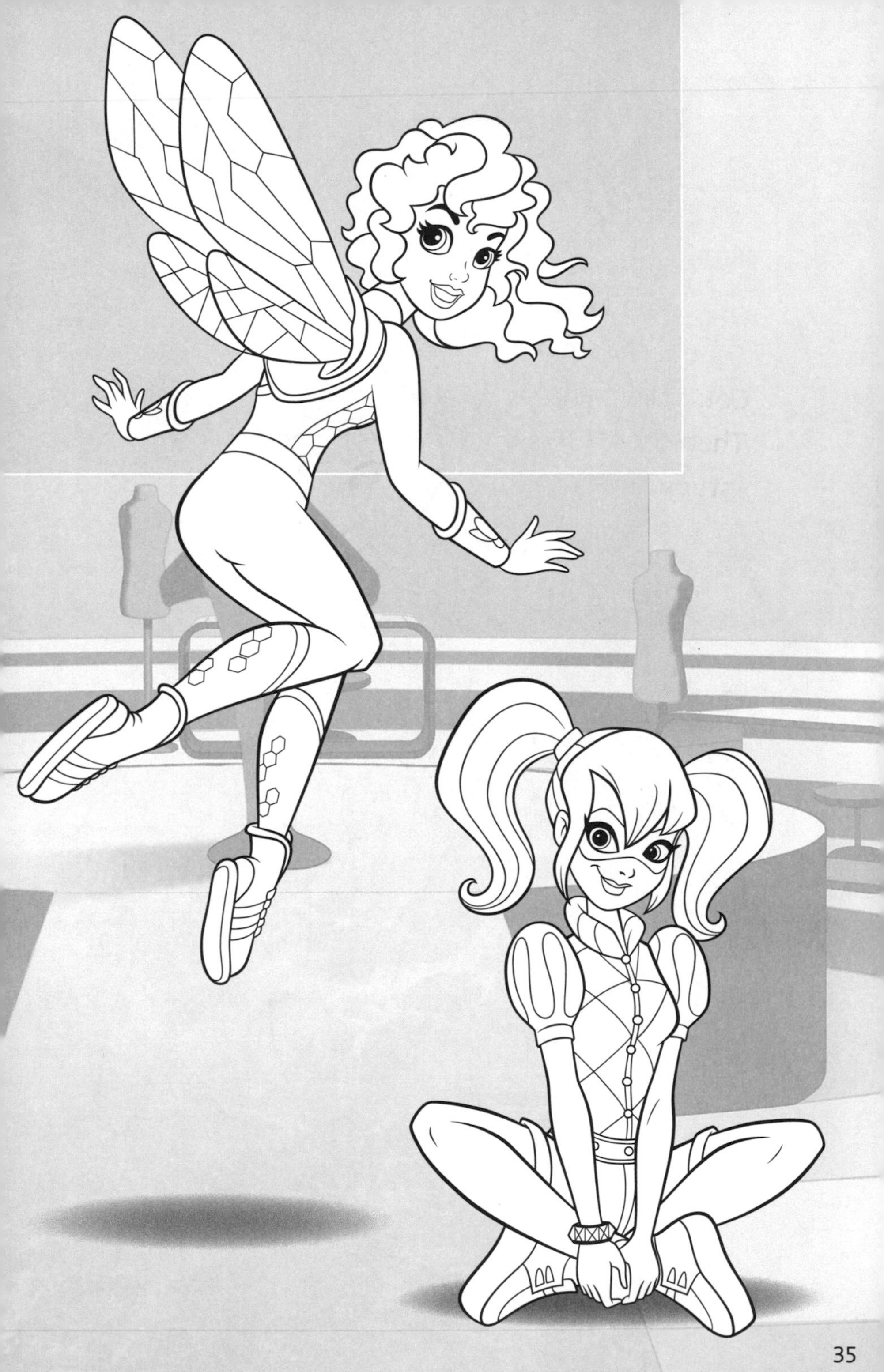

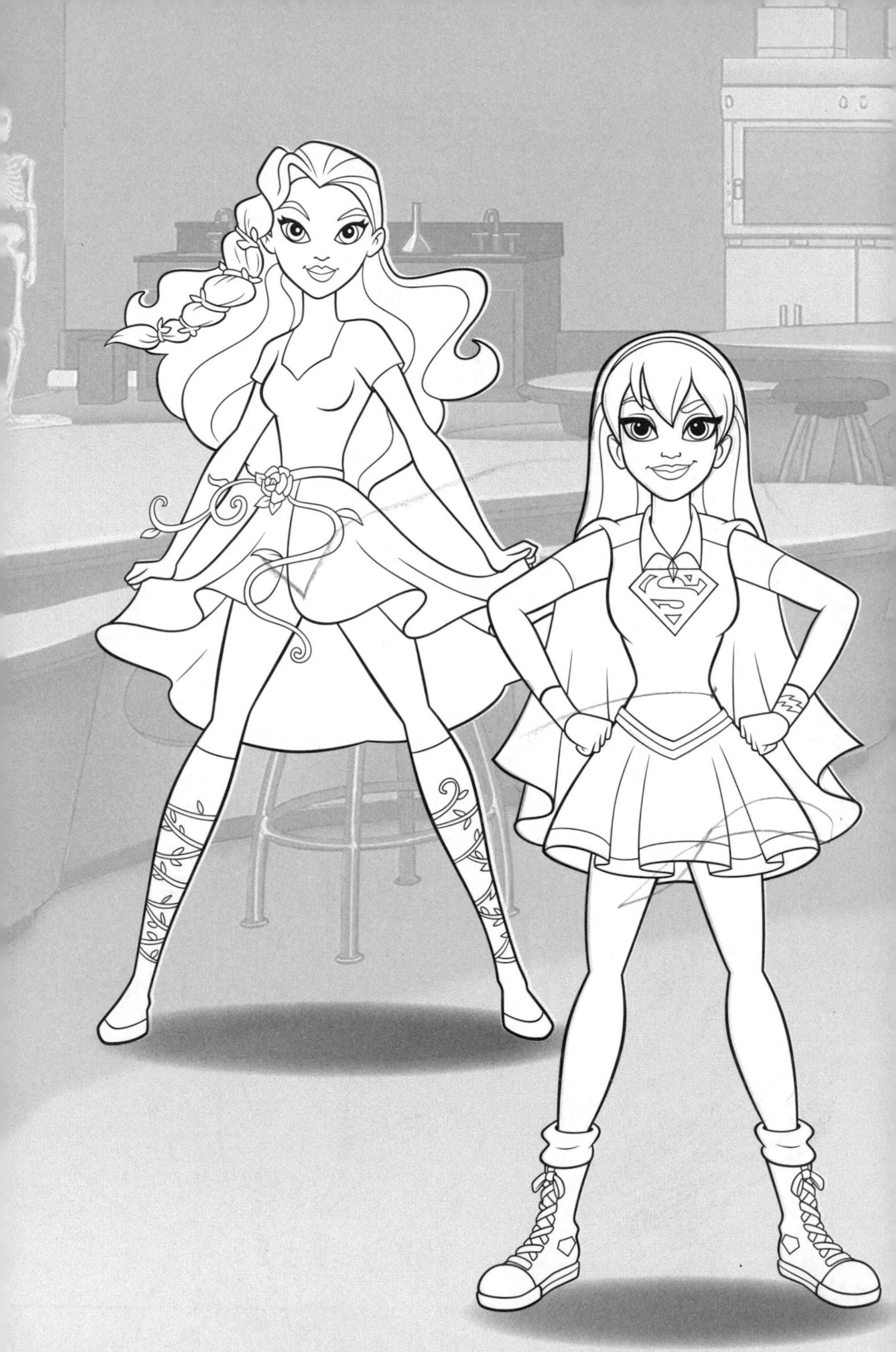

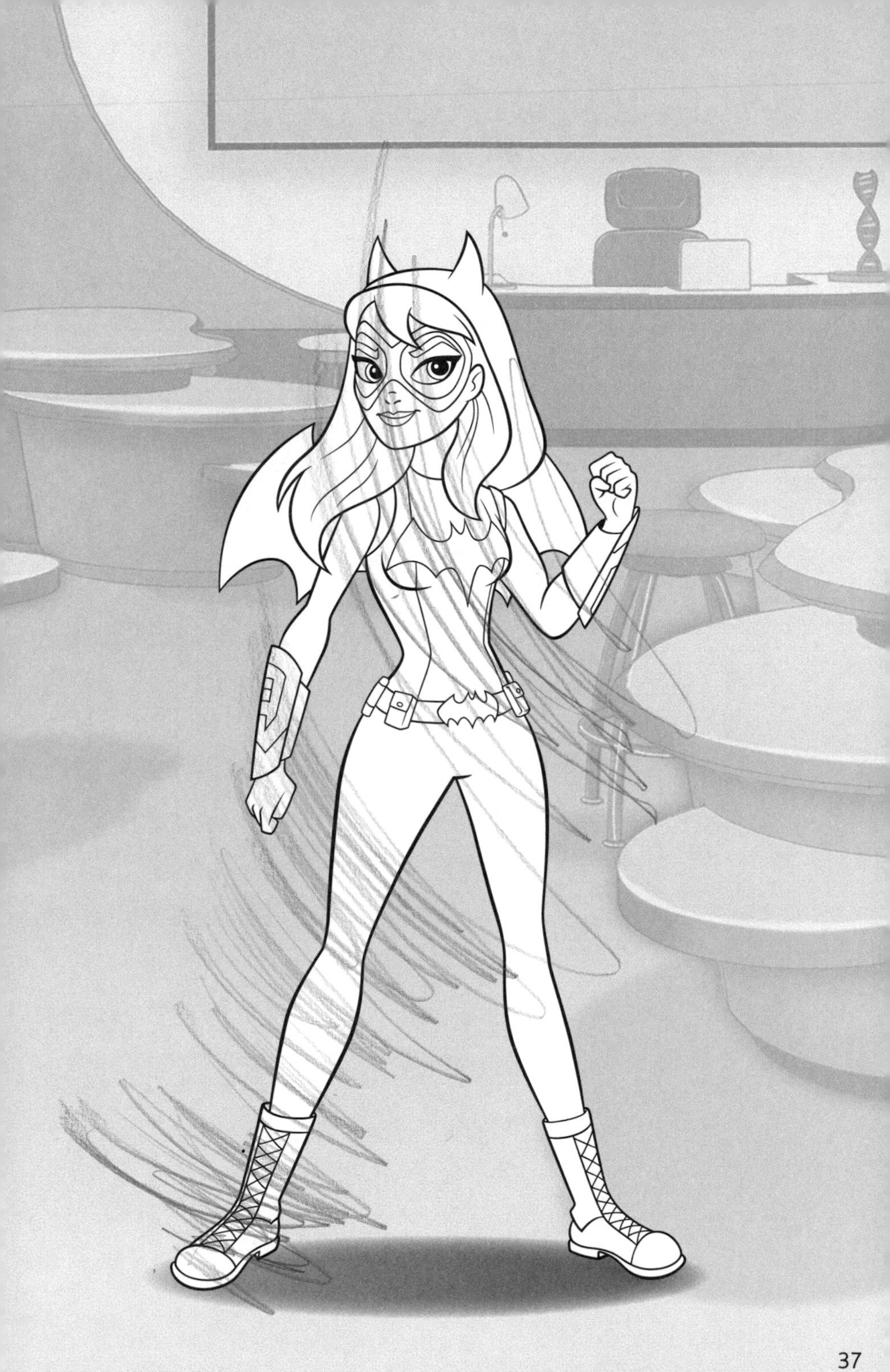

WEAPONOMICS

Would you prefer Katana's perfectly crafted samurai sword or Wonder Woman's Lasso of Truth? Invent and draw your own super hero weapons here and describe what they can be used for.

SHHS WALLS

Design some super hero posters
to decorate the halls of
Super Hero High School.

SUPER HERO CODE

Make up your own code by drawing a different symbol or mark for each letter. Then use this code every time you need to pass on a top-secret message.

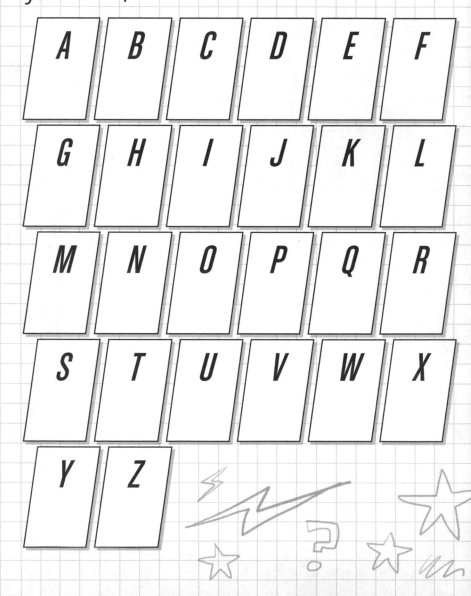

A B C D E F

G H I J K L

M N O P Q R

S T U V W X

Y Z

Practice writing a secret message in your code here.

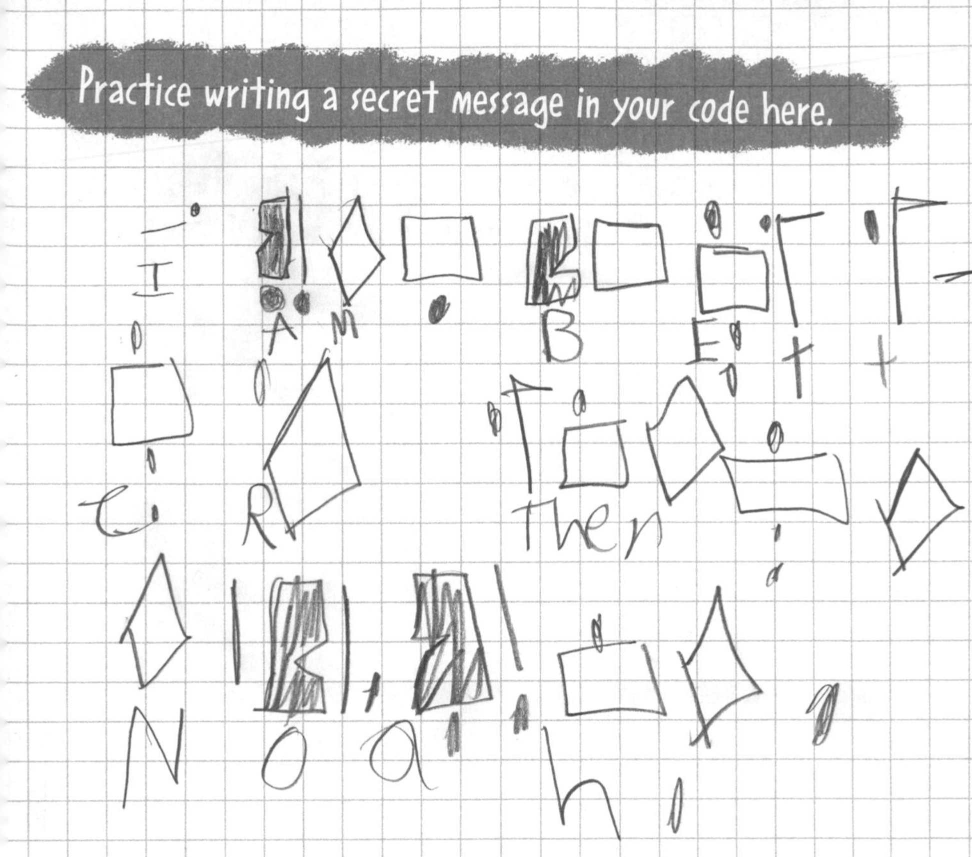
I
A M
B
E
C
R
then
N o a
h

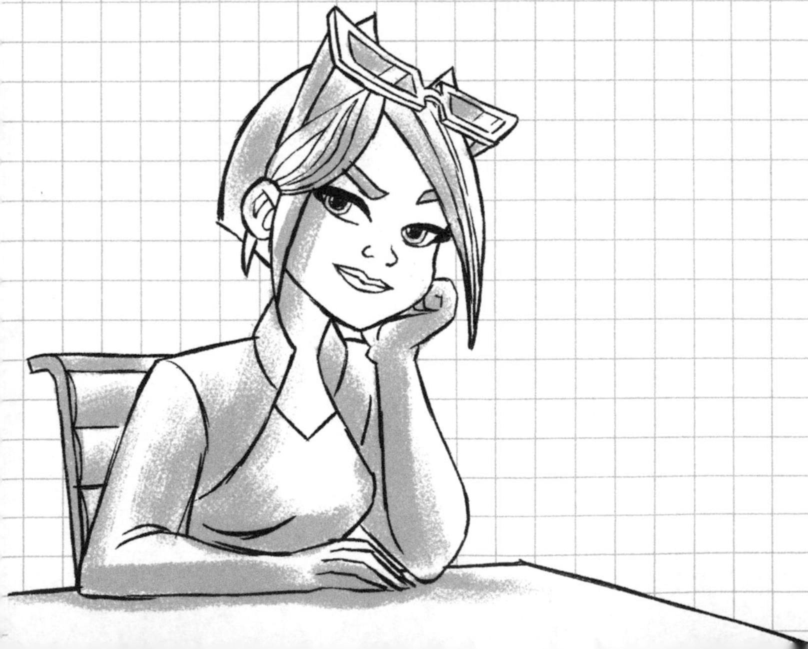

INVISIBLE FOR A DAY

Imagine you're invisible for the day.
Draw the adventures you would have!

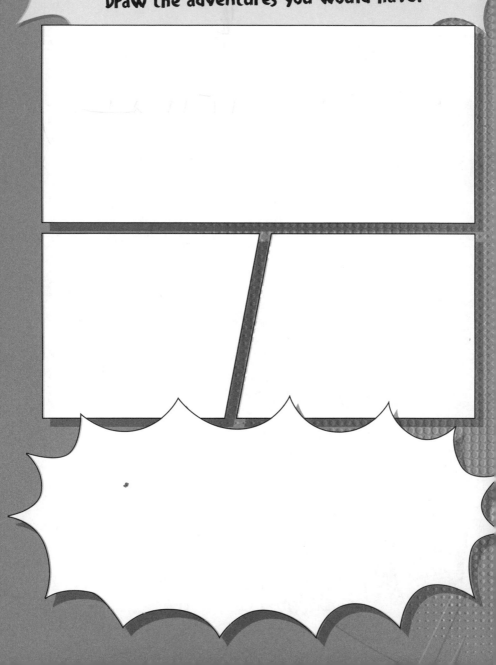

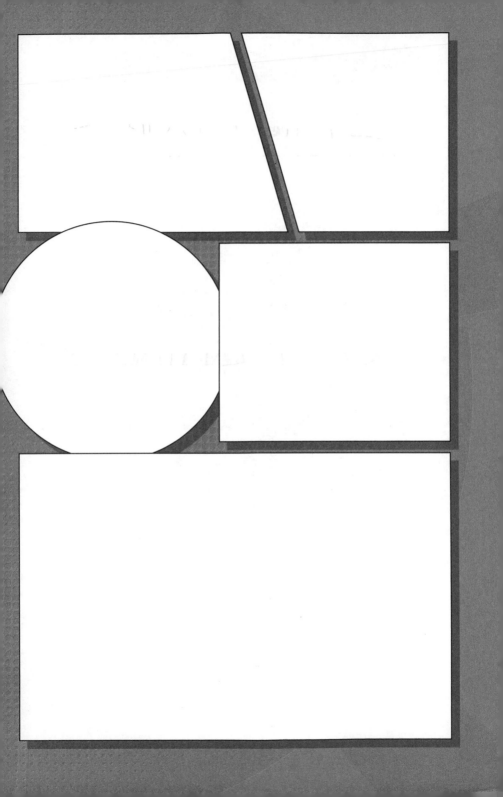

Brainpower

When you're a super hero-in-training, there's always so much to do and so little time to do it. Take a page out of Batgirl's brainy notebook and invent some incredible gadgets to help you with your everyday tasks. Remember, the galaxy's the limit when it comes to super hero inventions!

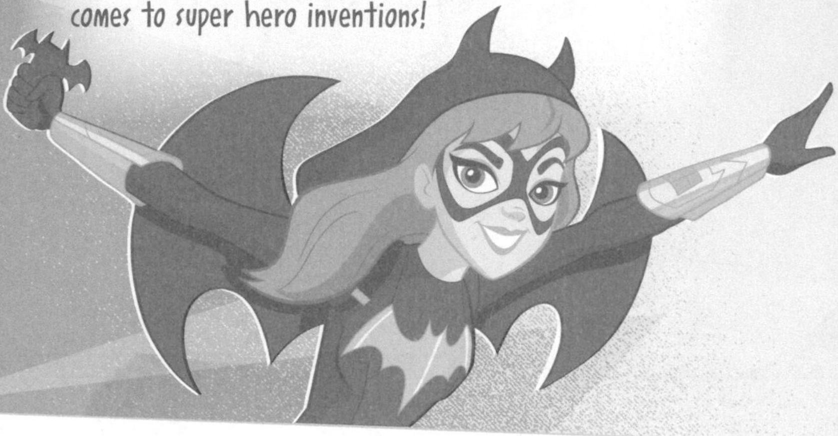

You're really late for class and your cape is totally covered in confetti after Harley's latest prank. Time to invent:

The

Oops! Even super heroes feel embarrassed sometimes. Time to disappear faster than the speed of light with:

The

You adore your noisy roommate, but you need to study and your headphones aren't working. Time to invent:

The

Your essay is due and the world needs saving from super-villains. Time to be in two places at once, using:

The

CAMPUS MAZE

Quick, you're late for class! Draw your way through campus, avoiding the booby traps along the way.

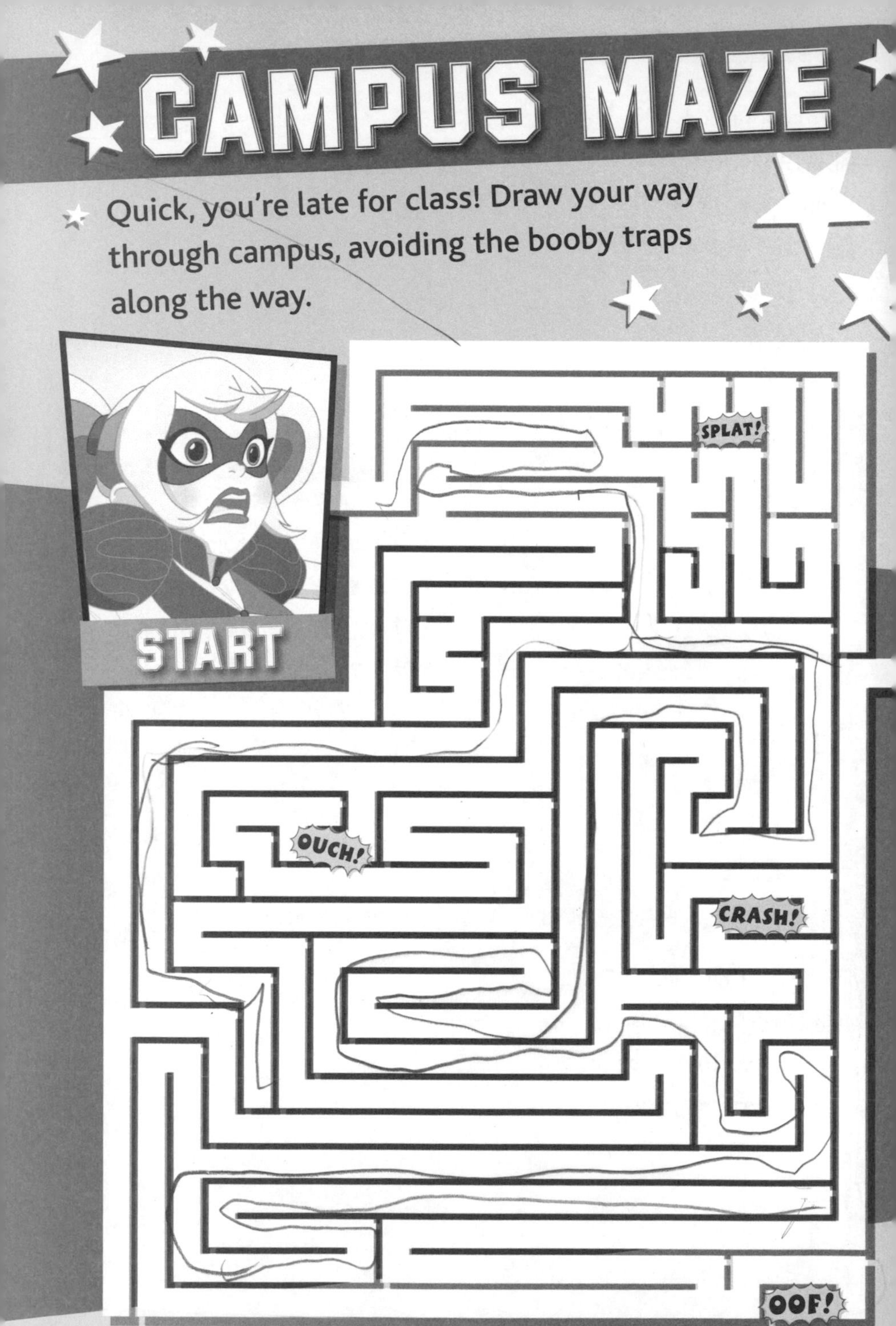
START
SPLAT!
OUCH!
CRASH!
OOF!

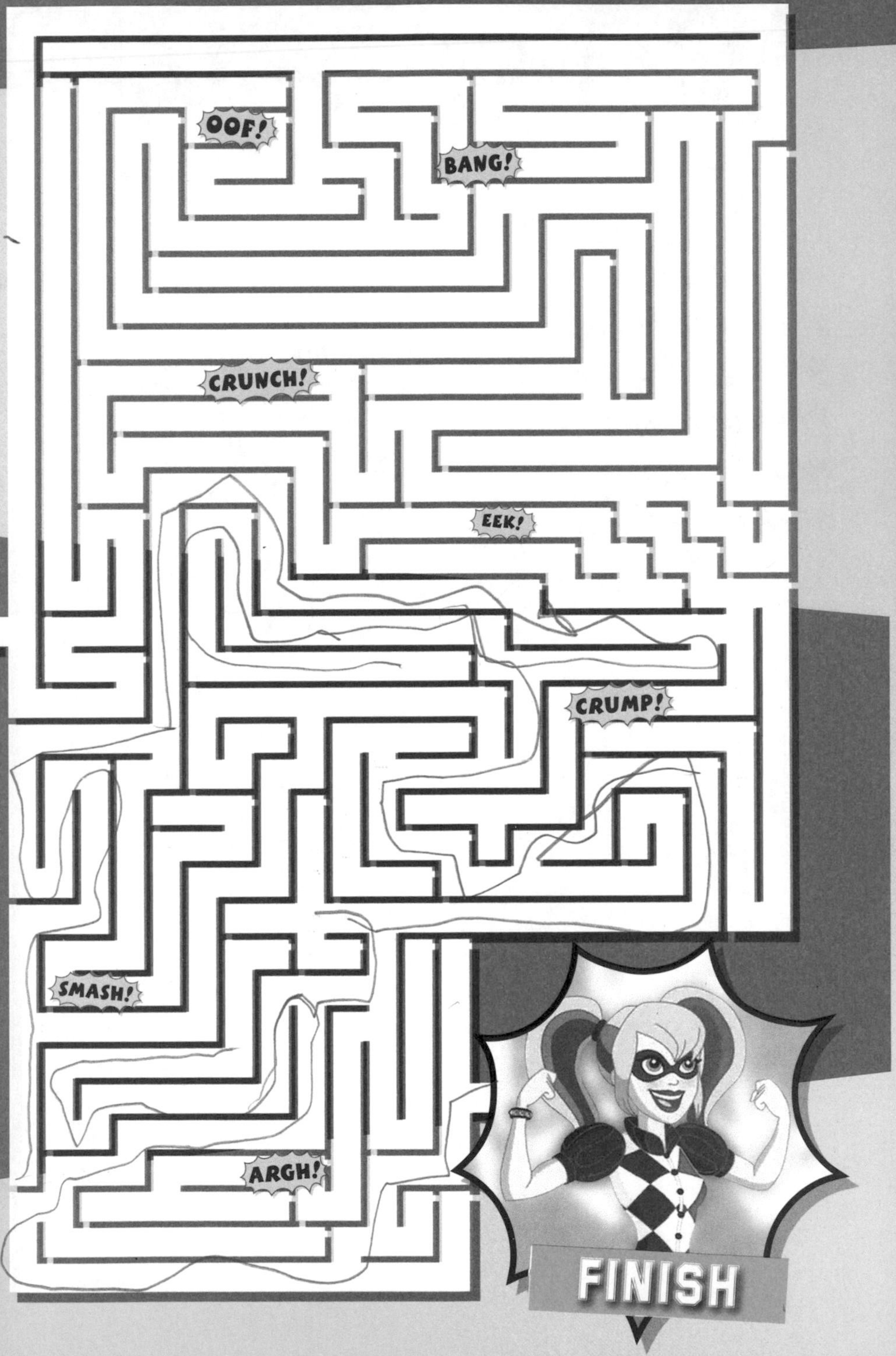
OOF!
BANG!
CRUNCH!
EEK!
CRUMP!
SMASH!
ARGH!
FINISH

ACCESSORIZE!

Crazy Quilt is helping his students accessorize their super hero costumes. Draw on some superpowered accessories and then color in the girls' outfits.

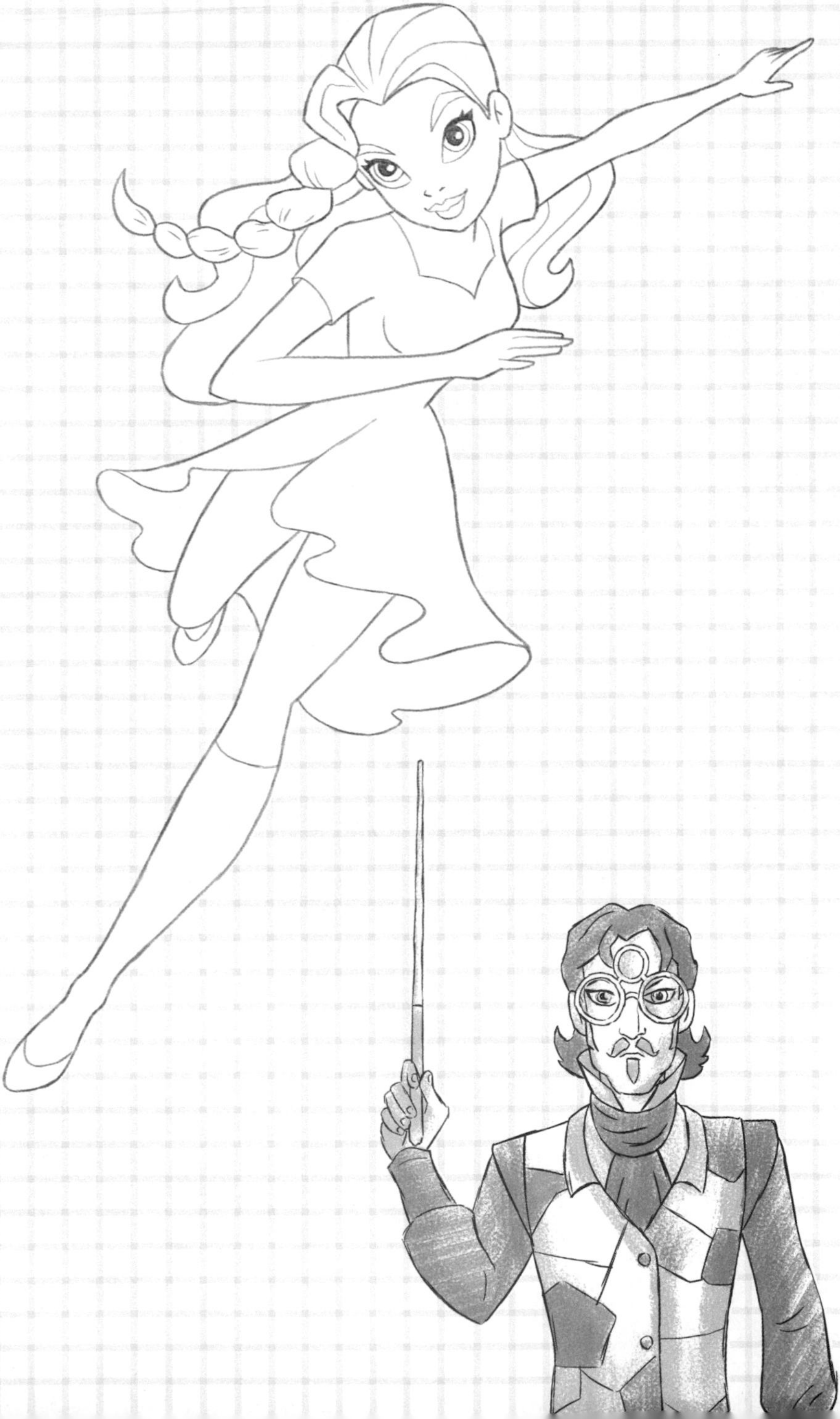

WHICH DC SUPER HERO GIRL IS MOST LIKE YOU?

Color in your end result,

YOU WOULD RATHER BE UP IN THE AIR THAN DOWN ON THE GROUND

YES NO

CREATIVITY IS VERY IMPORTANT TO YOU

YOU'RE MORE INTERESTED IN SCIENCE THAN IN BEING CREATIVE

YES NO YES NO

YOU'RE A NATURAL-BORN LEADER

YOU'D LOVE TO BE AN EXPERT WITH A SWORD

YOUR PERFECT DAY WOULD BE SPENT INVENTING GADGETS

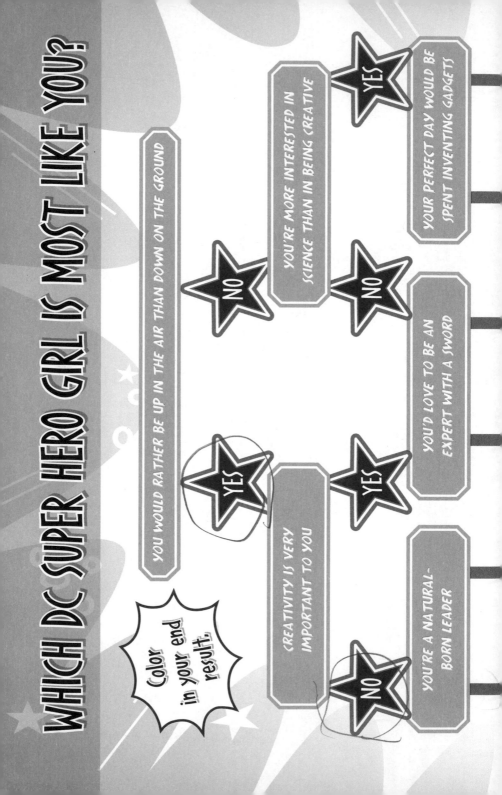

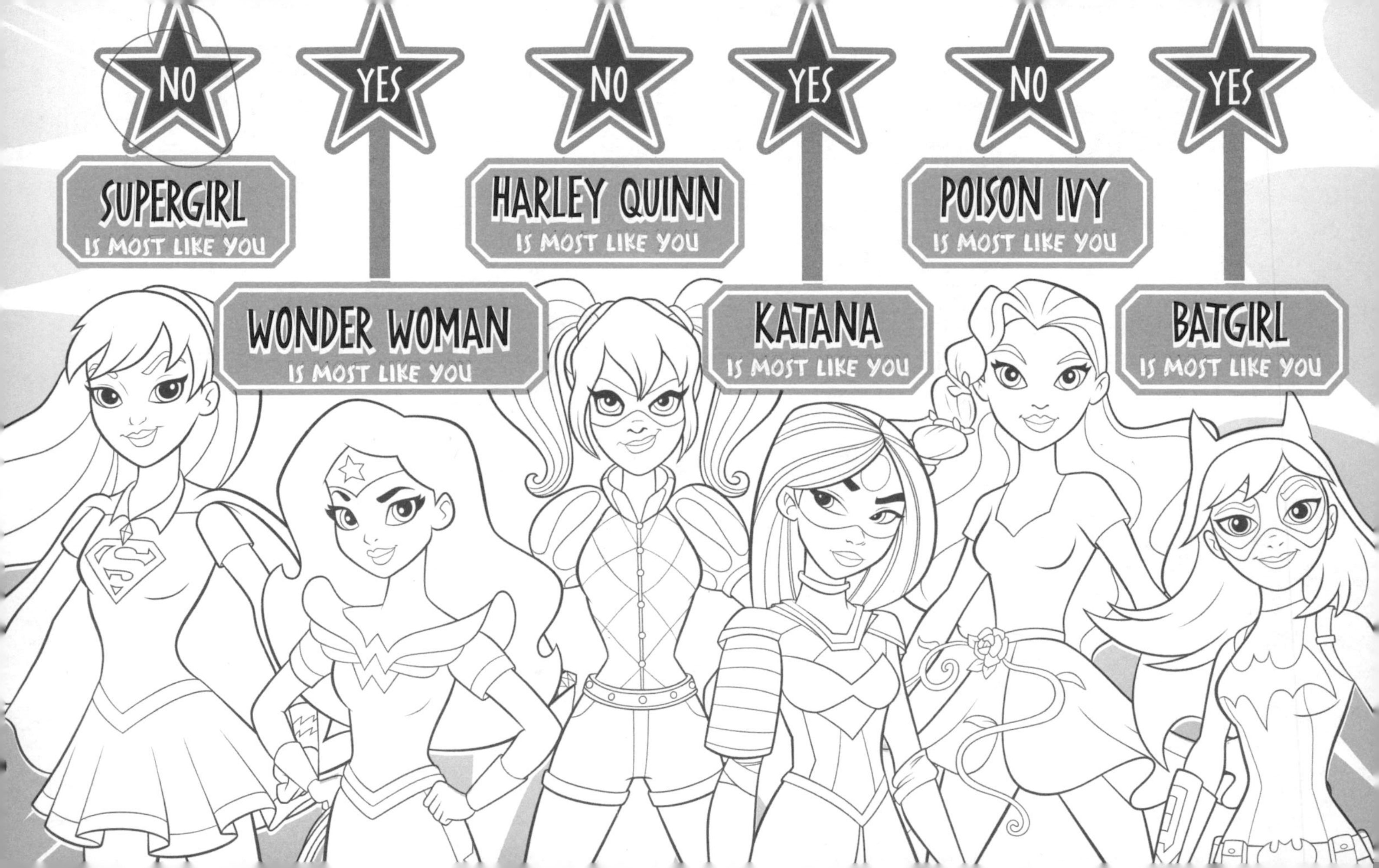
NO
YES
NO
YES
NO
YES
SUPERGIRL IS MOST LIKE YOU
WONDER WOMAN IS MOST LIKE YOU
HARLEY QUINN IS MOST LIKE YOU
KATANA IS MOST LIKE YOU
POISON IVY IS MOST LIKE YOU
BATGIRL IS MOST LIKE YOU

DIARY ENTRIES

Take a peep at some entries from the Super Hero Girls' diaries and see if you can match them to the right girl.

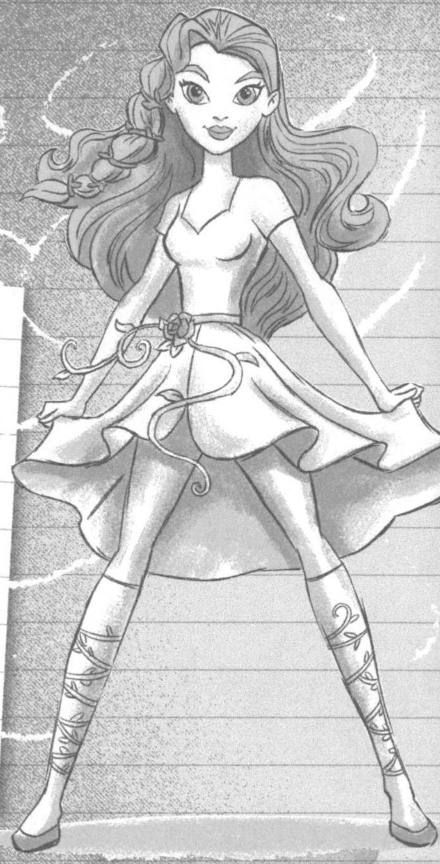

1

Yikes! Today was going so well. I had been flying around saving the day, but then, just as I was walking back to campus, I tripped and landed flat on my face! And to make it worse, EVERYONE was watching! I'd only gone and tied my bootlaces together. And now I realize that they must've been like that all day! Oh well, at least I didn't land on anyone.

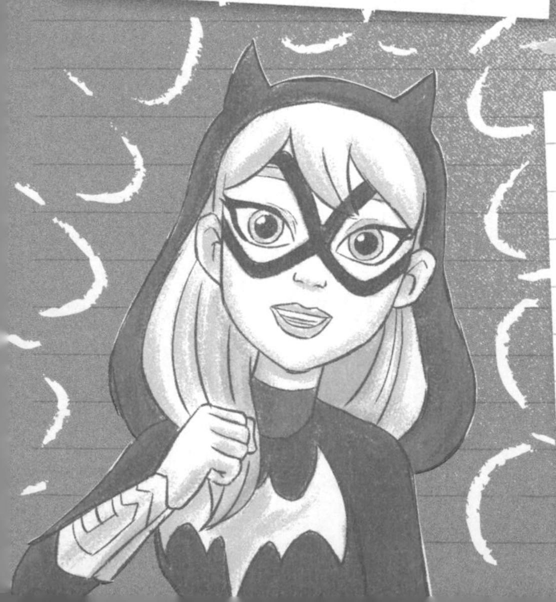

2

Today I was told to join a new after-school club. The thing is, none of them really interest me. Band Club, Model United Planets, Yearbook Team . . . they're just not my thing. I wonder if there's a science club around somewhere? That would be more like it.

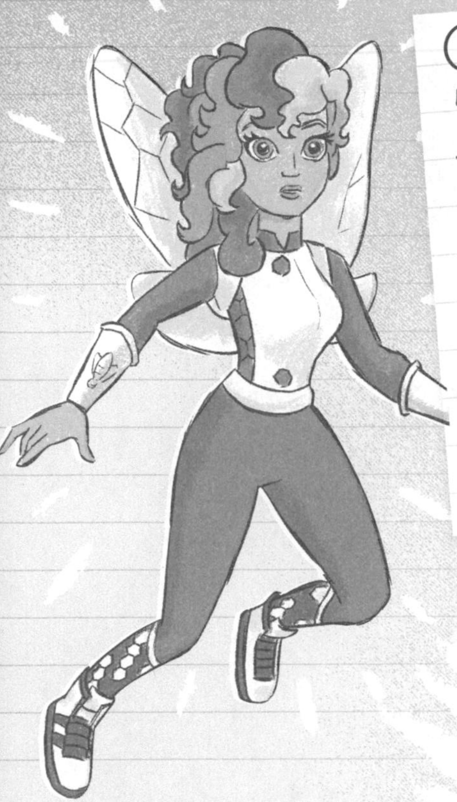

(4)

I'm pretty sure there's something suspicious going on in the dorm room next to mine. No one has come or gone from it for days, but I can hear strange beeping noises coming from inside and they're keeping me awake. I must invent something to help me to investigate . . .

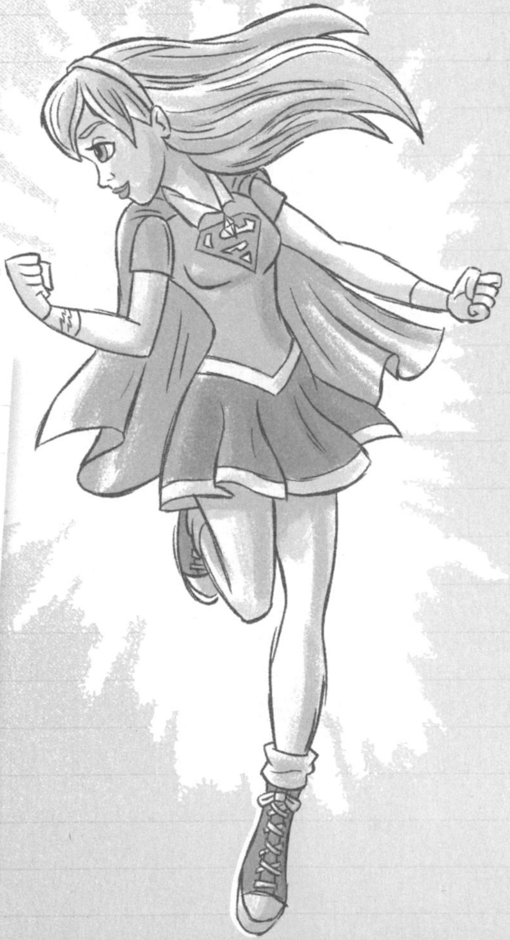

(3)

I'm having a small problem right now. There's a malfunction with the microchip in my earbuds, which is making me shrink uncontrollably. Luckily, I think I've found out how to fix it. I just need to stay big for a little bit—uh-oh! Here we go again . . .

5

Today was, like, totally hilarious. I set up a whole load of booby traps around school and then filmed everyone falling for them. Wondy's was the best—she looked sooooo embarrassed!

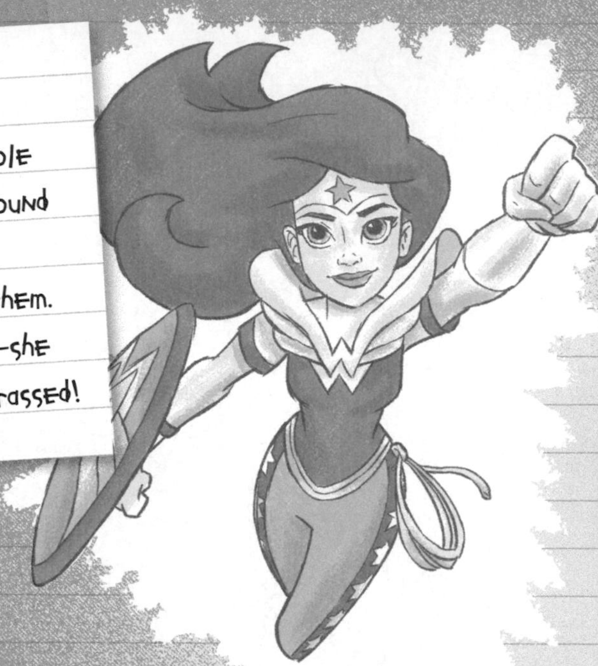

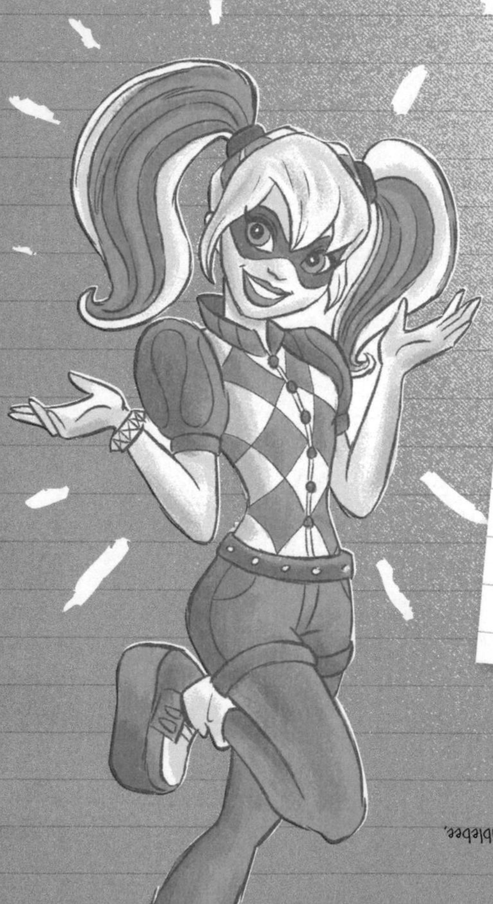

6

I'm trying really hard to focus on fitting in at SHHS and making the entire world a better and safer place at the same time. Sometimes, though, when your roommate is constantly playing little tricks on you, one mission definitely seems a lot easier than the other!

Answers: 1 is written by Supergirl, 2 by Poison Ivy, 3 by Bumblebee, 4 by Batgirl, 5 by Harley Quinn, and 6 by Wonder Woman.

Use this page to write or record an entry from your own diary that says a lot about you.

THE HERO OF THE MONTH IS . . .

Super Hero High is pleased to announce that the Hero of the Month is . . . YOU! Fill in your details below for this impressive award. You're the super hero who has shown helpfulness and selflessness and acted as an outstanding role model. You're awesome!

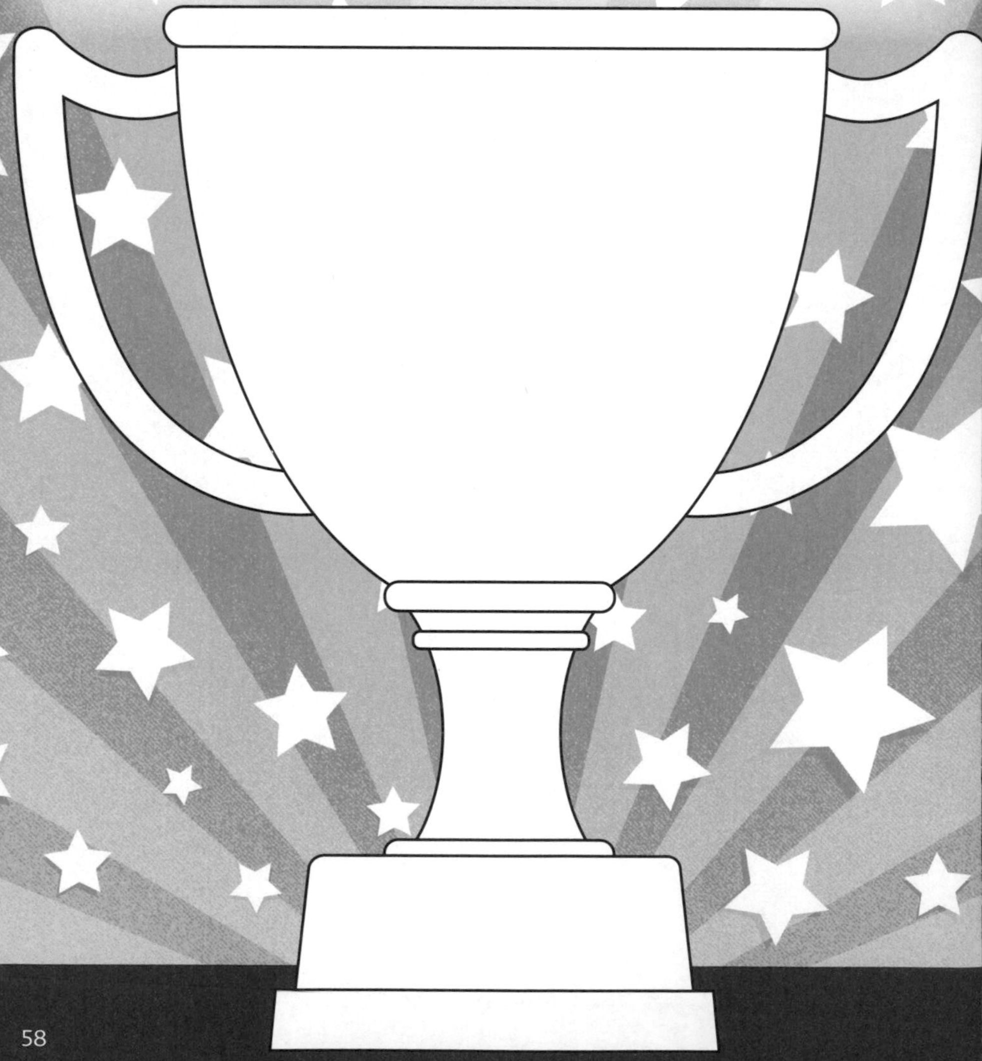

MY TOP 10 SUPER HERO TUNES

What would be your super hero theme song when it's time for you to come to the rescue? List your top 10 super hero tunes here.

Strike a Pose

You've taken to the skies! What do you look like when you fly? Draw yourself in a powerful pose high up in the sky. What can you see down below?

My BFFs

Use these pages to draw and stick in pictures of you and your best friends hanging out in super hero style.

MY SUPER HERO SECRETS

Keep your secrets safe from villainous eyes here.

(It'd be an especially good idea to write them in your super hero secret code!)

CLASS CLOWN PRANKS

If you were Harley Quinn, what joke or prank would you play on your classmates? Draw or describe it here.

QUICK THINKING

Catwoman's trapped underground! Can you help her find her way to the surface?

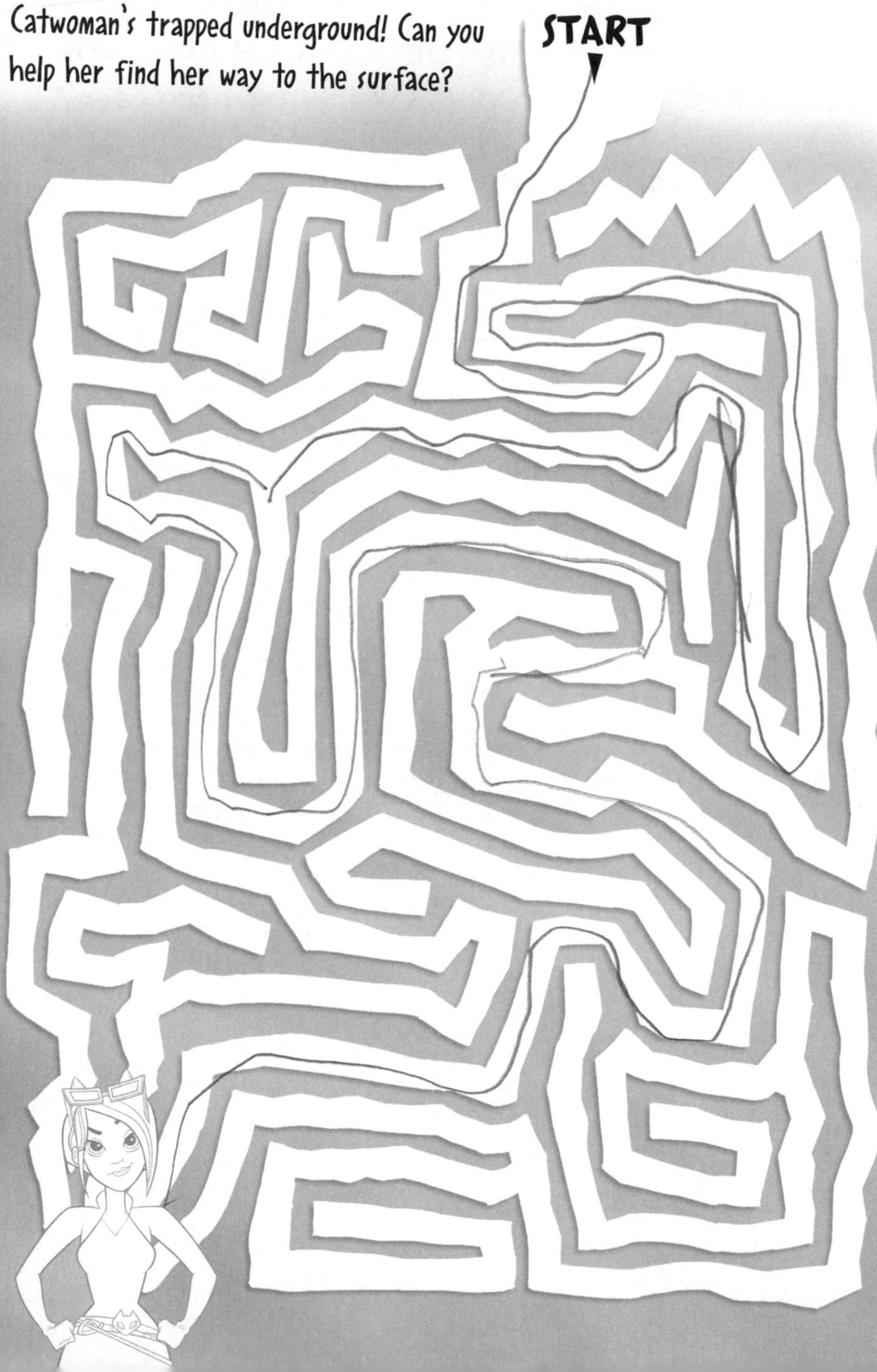
START

SUPER HERO ESSAY

It's essay time! Answer the following questions to help you to write your own super hero essay.

What's it like being a super hero?

What is the most heroic thing you've ever done?

If you had unlimited superpowers, what would you do with them?

Describe a typical day in your super hero life.

MY TOP 10 AMBITIONS . . .

What are the top 10 things you would most like to achieve with your superpowers? Remember, dream big! You can do anything you set your mind to.

1. _____

2. _____

3. _____

4. _____

5. _____

6. _____

7. _____

8. _____

9. _____

10. _____

. . . AND HOW TO ACHIEVE THEM

Now that you've identified your super hero goals, it's time to work out how you'll achieve them.

1. --

2. --

3. --

4. --

5. --

6. --

7. --

8. --

9. --

10. --

Poison Ivy, How Does

Draw Poison Ivy's garden here.

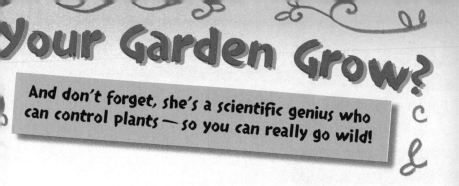

Your Garden Grow?

And don't forget, she's a scientific genius who can control plants — so you can really go wild!

SUPER HERO SLEEPOVER

Fill in all the details to host your
own super hero sleepover.

Who's Coming?

Design your invitation here. You can even photocopy, scan, or take a picture of it, and then send it to each of the people on your *Who's Coming?* list!

SLEEPOVER PREP

There's so much to do before everyone arrives!
Make sure there's lots of super hero fun for all.

Snacks:

Drinks:

Games to play:

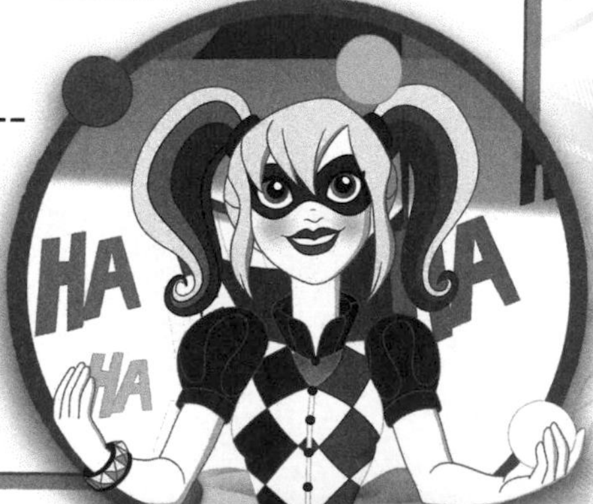
HA
HA
HA

 Someone needs saving at your super hero sleepover! What happened, and how can you use the things you've provided for your party to save the day? Super heroes have to be resourceful!

FLYERS' ED

What can you do while in flight? Loop the loop, save an airplane, dodge fireworks? Make up your own obstacle course here to challenge even the most daredevil flyers! How many people of Metropolis can you save on the way? Doodle what you dream up!

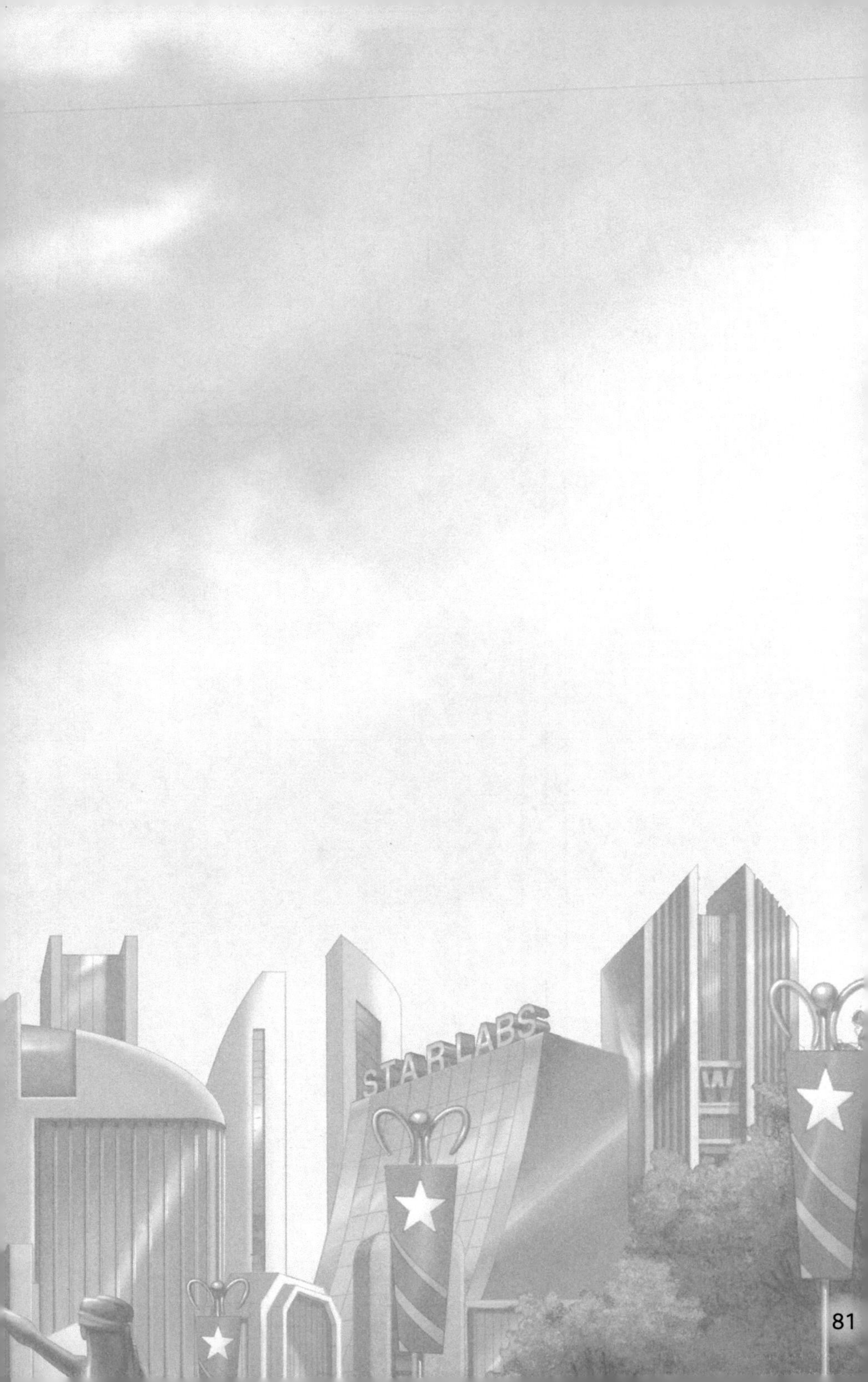
STAR LABS

What's in Your Locker?

Draw it here.

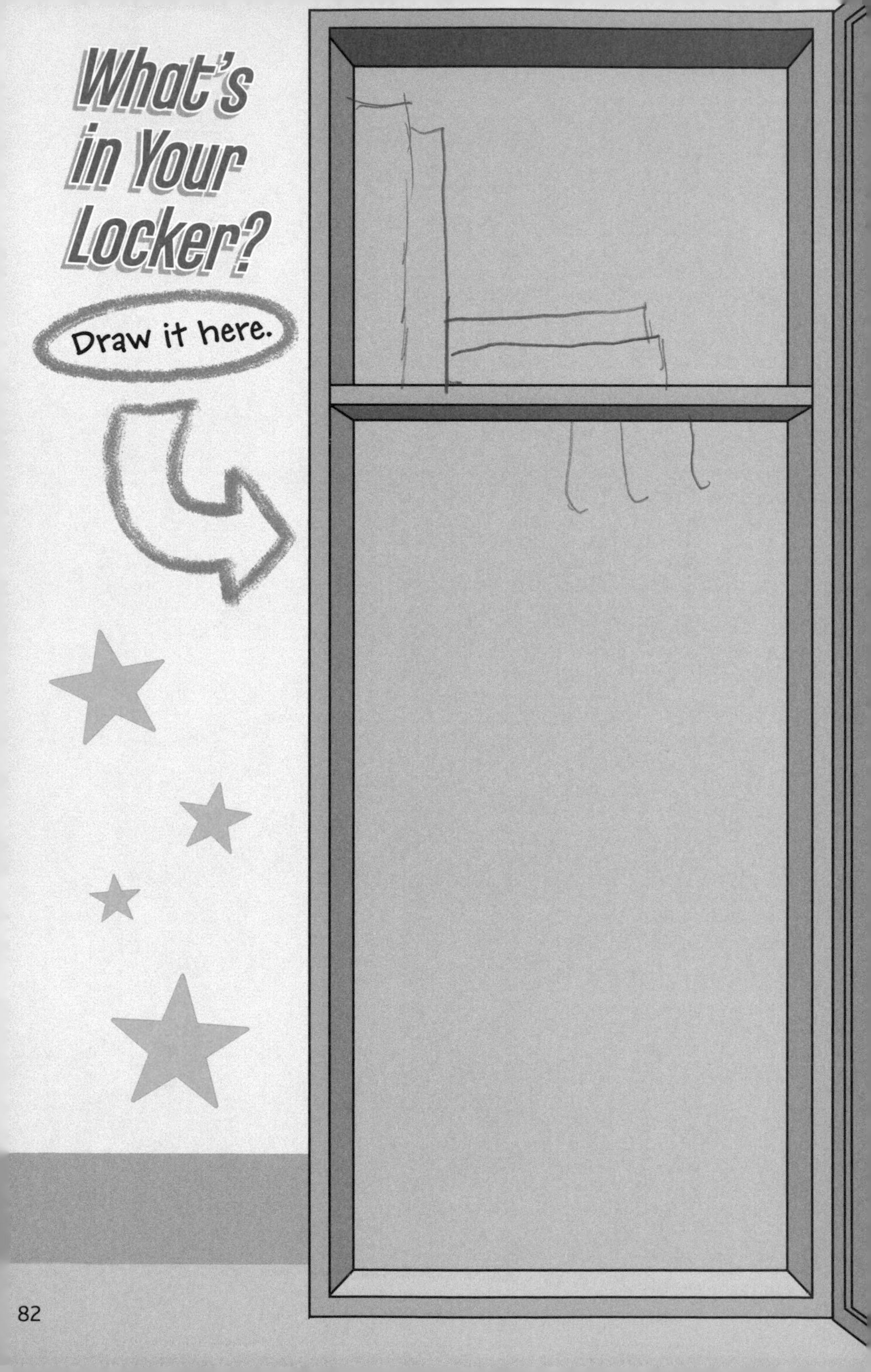

Quick Assignment:

BRAIN BUZZ

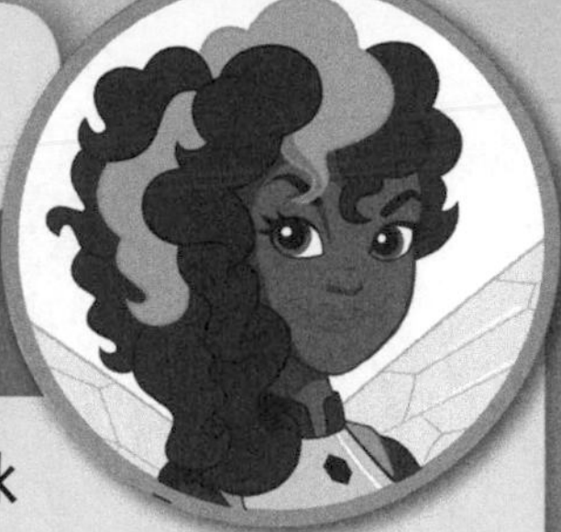

Bumblebee loves her trademark symbol. Design a logo of your own.

WHAT WOULD WONDER WOMAN DO?

Imagine you're Wonder Woman for a day. What would you do if you had her skills and powers? Fill these pages with all your adventures.

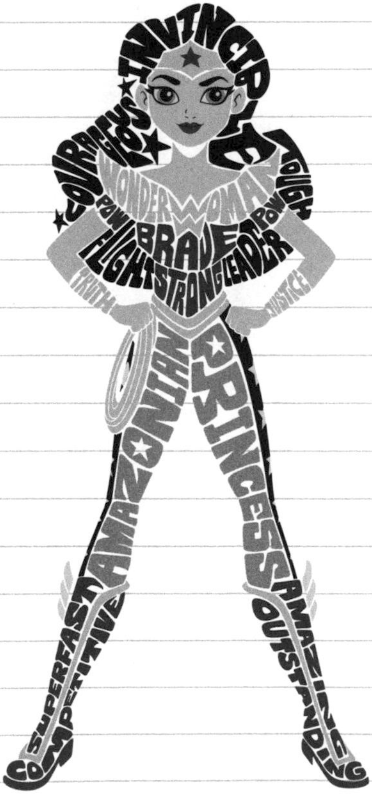

INVINCIBLE
WONDER WOMAN
TOUGH
BRAVE
FLIGHT
STRONG
LEADER
TRUTH
JUSTICE
AMAZONIAN
PRINCESS
SUPERFAST
COMPETITIVE
AMAZING
OUTSTANDING

TEAMWORK

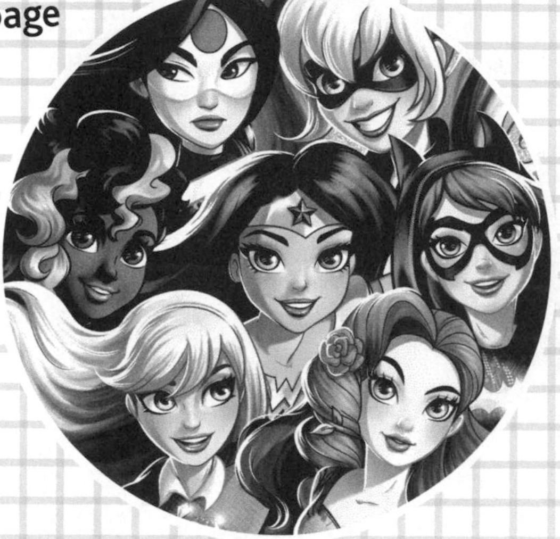

Cut out the opposite page and fold it along the lines as shown in the diagram. Then grab some friends and take turns drawing on each section and create your own new (and awesome) super hero!

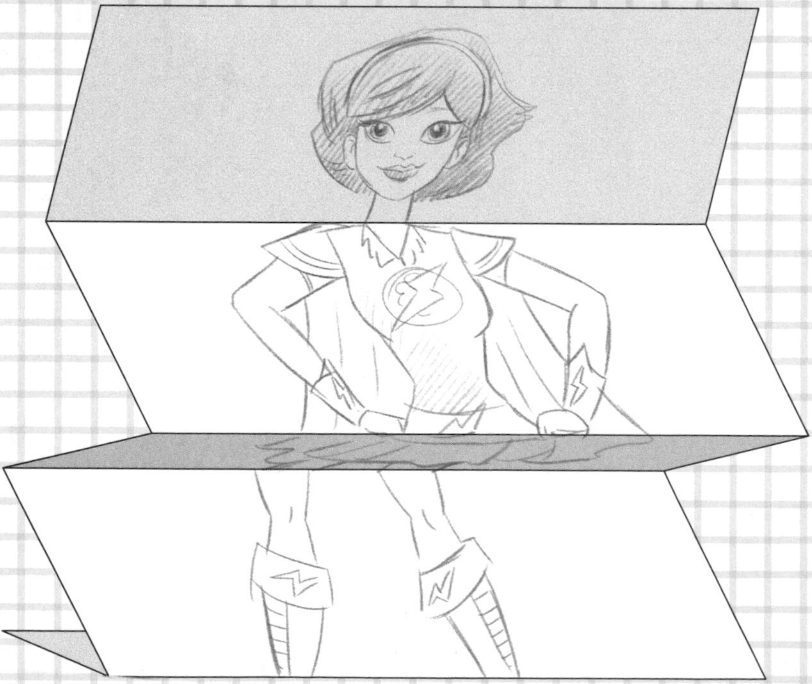

STARRY-EYED

Use patterns, colors, shapes, and doodles to make each of the stars on this page totally unique.

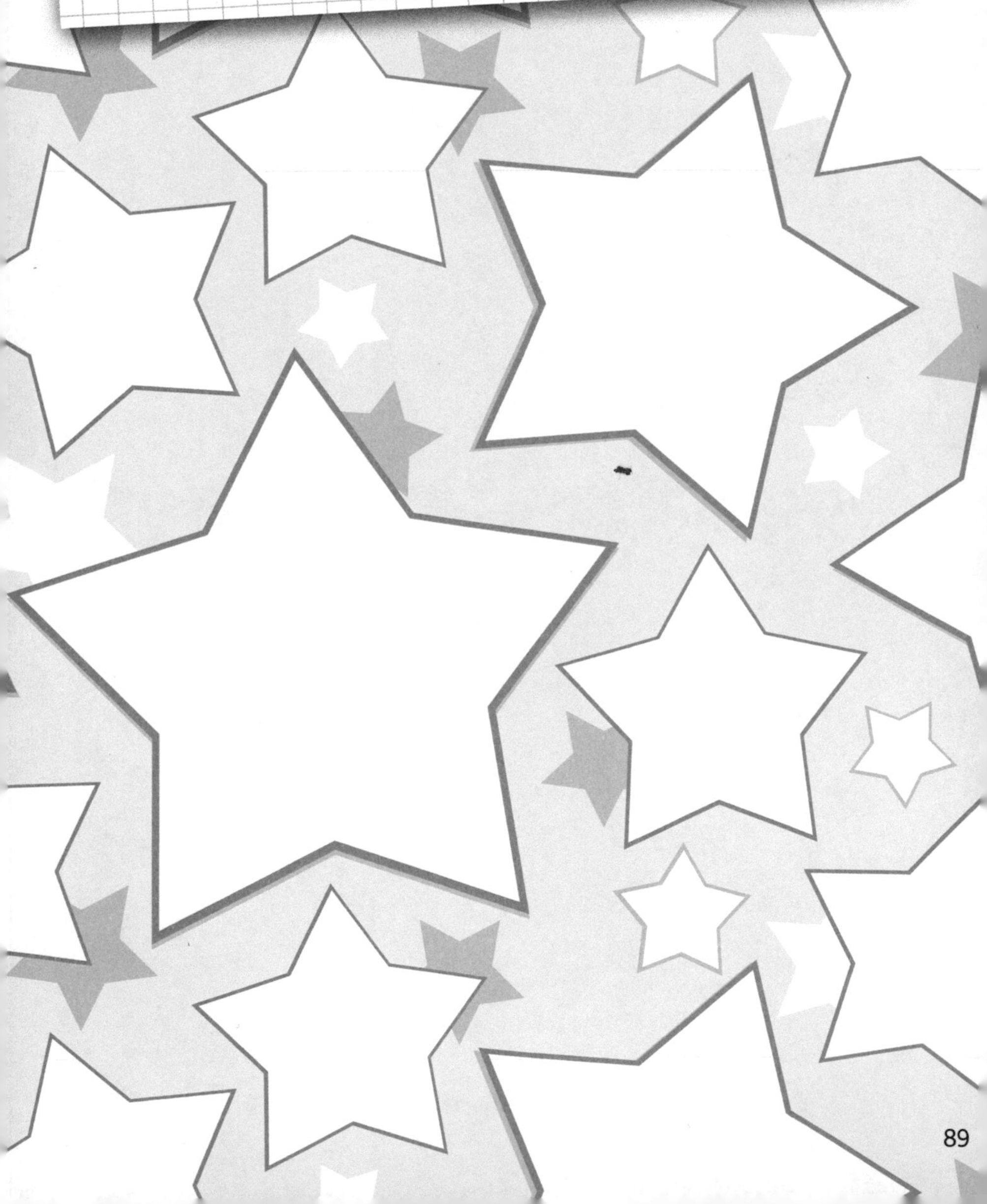

Dream BIG

What are the super hero girls dreaming about?

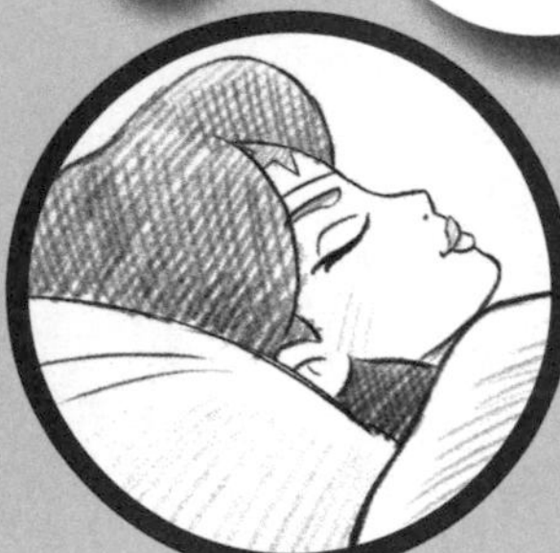

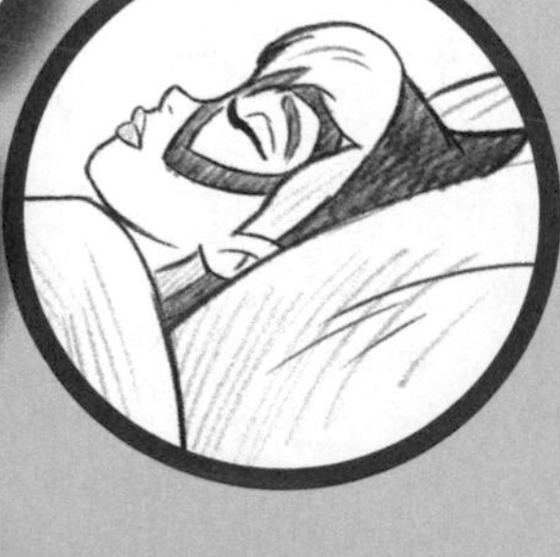

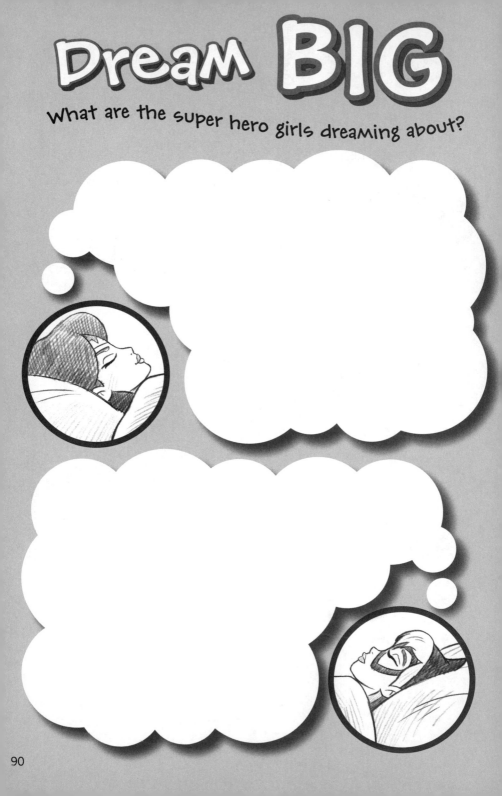

The What-If Game

Get ready to leap into action and save the day
by finishing these super hero sentences!

If I had Bumblebee's ability to shrink, I would:

If a tornado was headed toward Super Hero High, I would:

If I was busy eating my favorite food and a save-the-day alarm sounded, I would:

If there was a mountain standing in my way, I would:

If my friend was about to trip, I would:

SUPER SNACK TIME

Every super hero girl needs food fuel! What are your favorite snacks to keep your energy up?

Draw them here.

My Ultimate Meal

This morning you saved the staff of Capes & Cowls Café from a super-villain who was trying to steal all the money from the till. The café owner is so grateful, he's offered to make your favorite meal for you! So what's on the menu?

CAPES & COWLS CAFÉ

Appetizer

....

....

Main Course

....

....

Dessert

....

....

SUPER HERO SELFIE

Nice work—you've saved the world with your super hero friends! Draw or tape a picture of all of you celebrating here.

GIRL POWER!

Take a look at this picture, then turn the page and try to draw as much of it as you can, using your powerful memory!

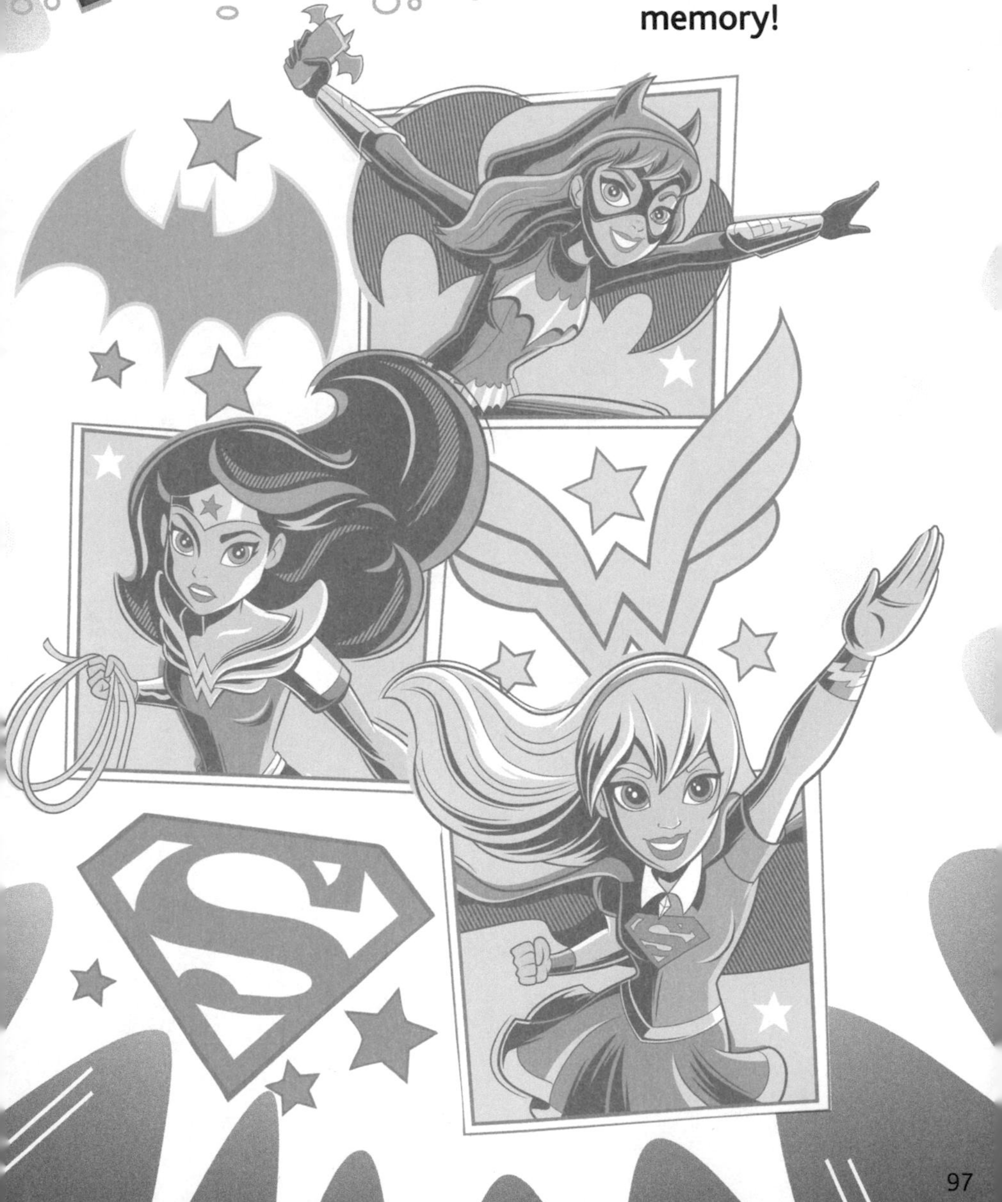

My Top 10 Embarrassing Moments

Oops! Use this page to record your goof-ups. We all have them— even super heroes.

1. _____

2. _____

3. _____

4. _____

5. _____

6. _____

7. _____

8. _____

9. _____

10. _____

Quick Assignment:

IT'S ALL IN THE DETAILS

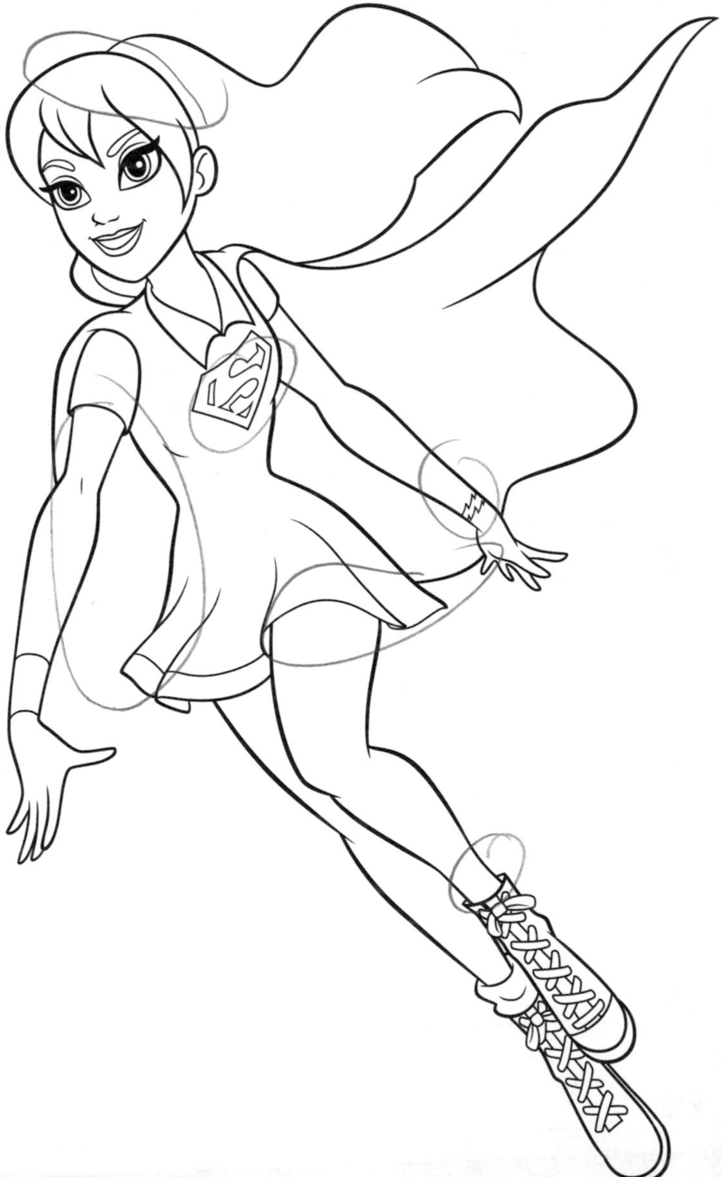

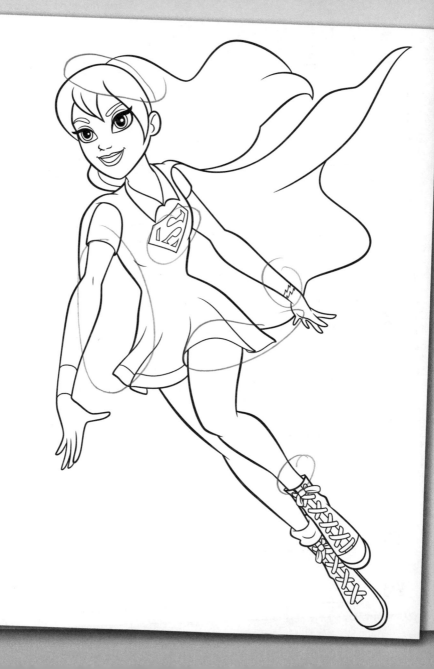

You'll need patience and a keen eye to make these two pictures of Supergirl identical. Do you have what it takes?

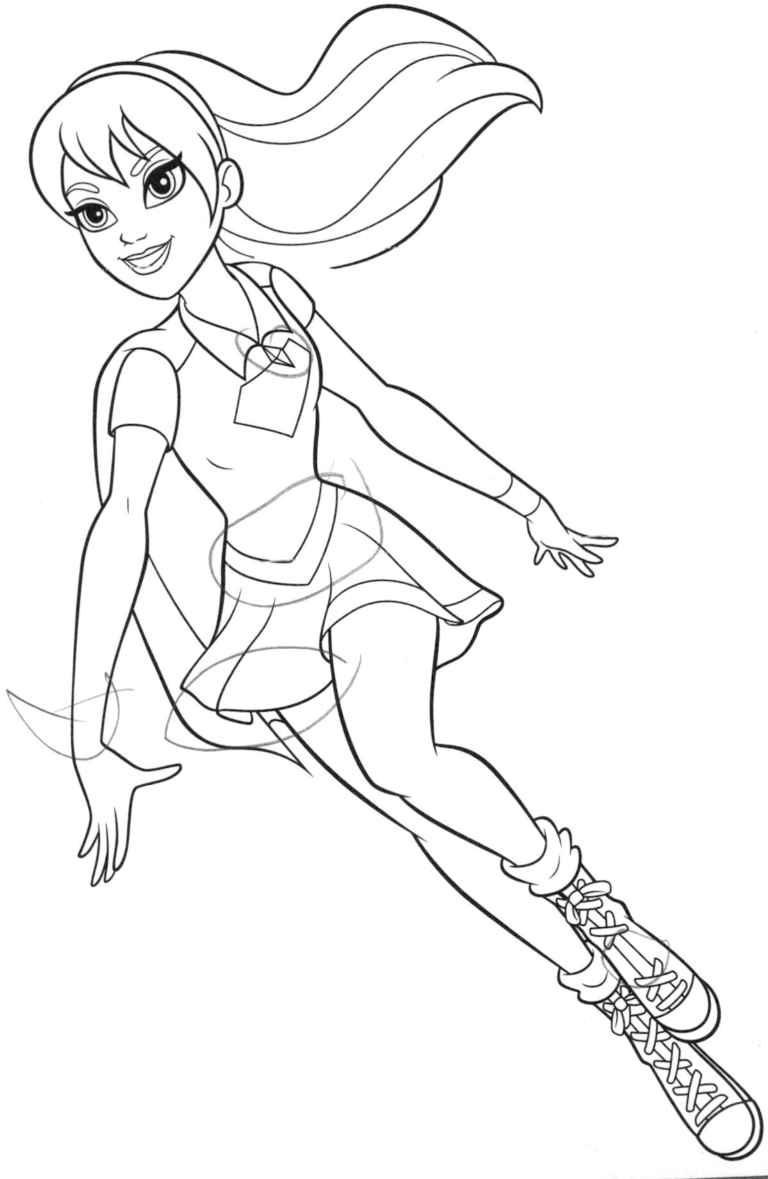

TARGET PRACTICE

Challenge a friend to a game of squares. Grab a different-colored pen or pencil each and take turns drawing a line to connect two dots. The aim of the game is to make as many squares as possible. Each time you complete a square, add your initials. The person with the most squares wins!

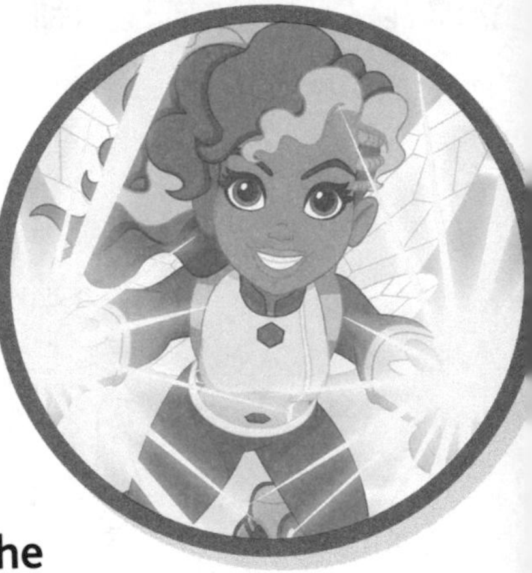

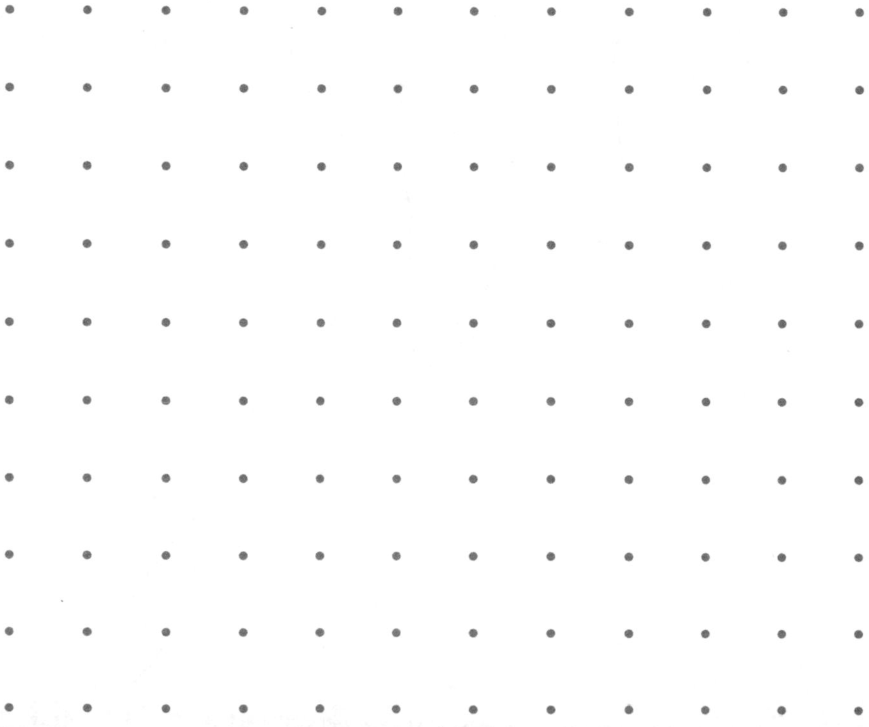

https://www.

SUPER HERO BLOG

Design your own super hero blog page. What would it be about, and what would it look like?

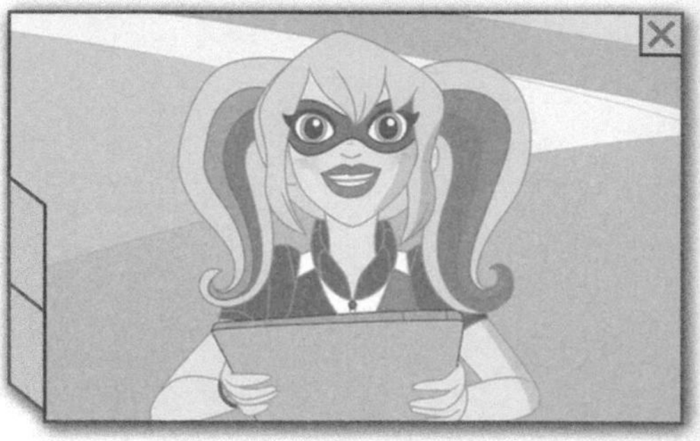

Search

Pow! BANG! Shh!

Write or draw what you think might have happened in each of the bursts below.

BOOM!

SPLAT!

WHEEE!

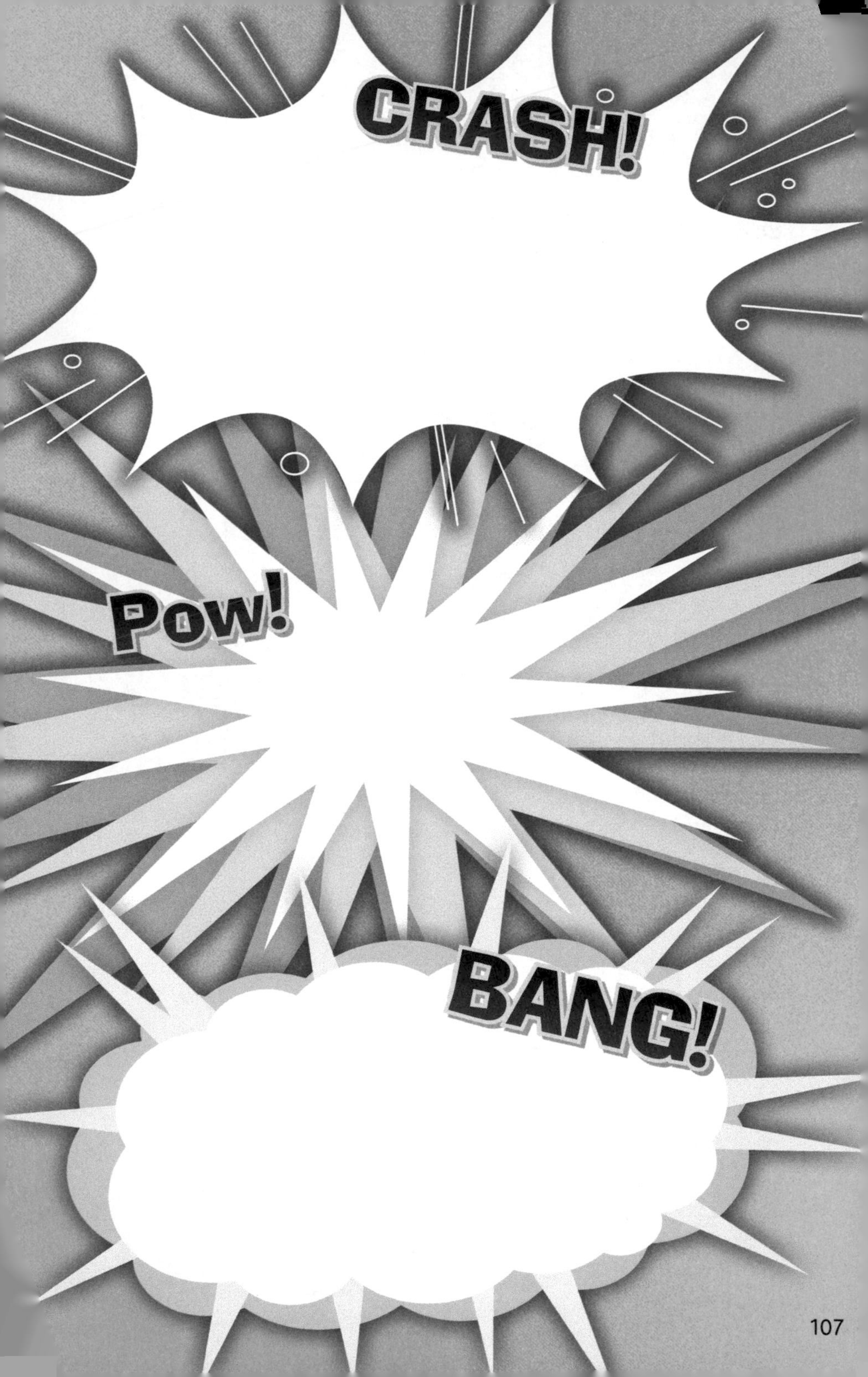
CRASH!
Pow!
BANG!

SUPER HERO SELFIE

Draw or tape a picture of yourself in each scene.

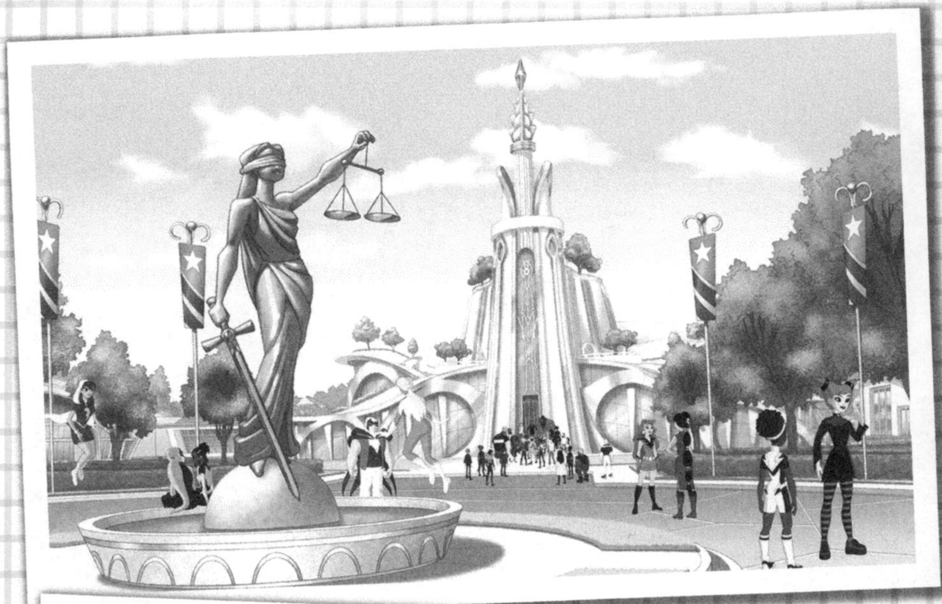

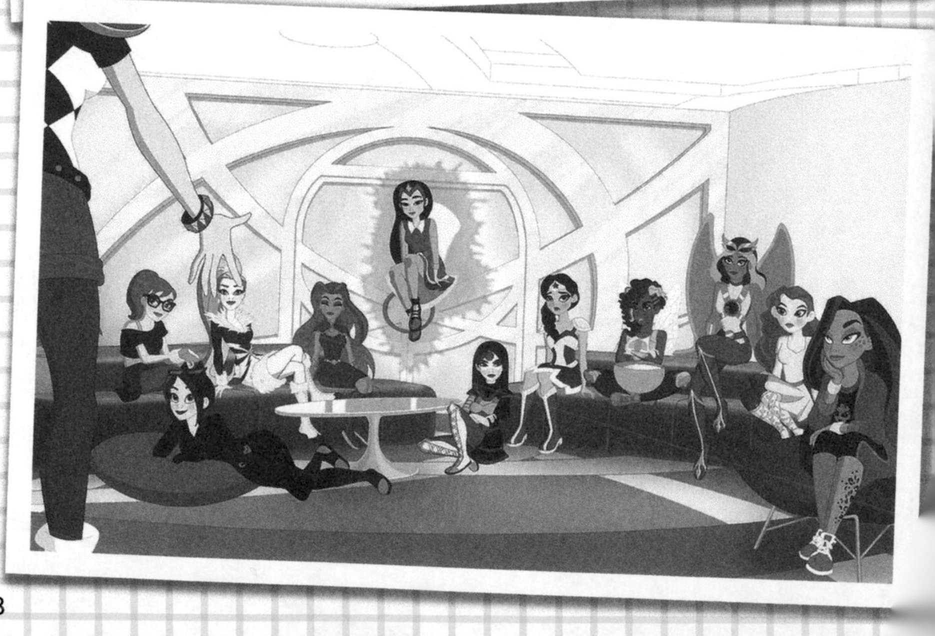

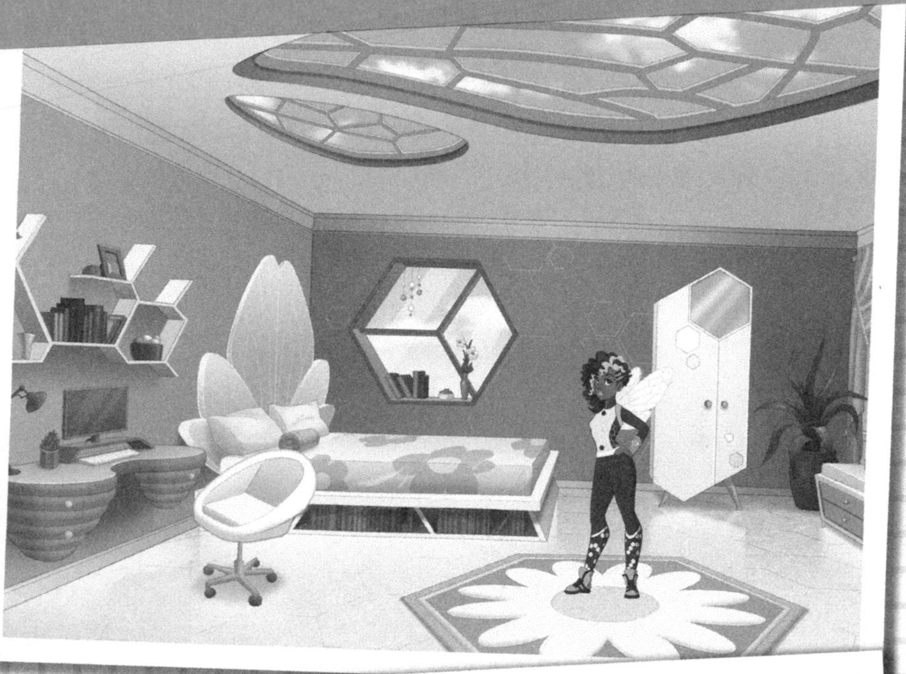

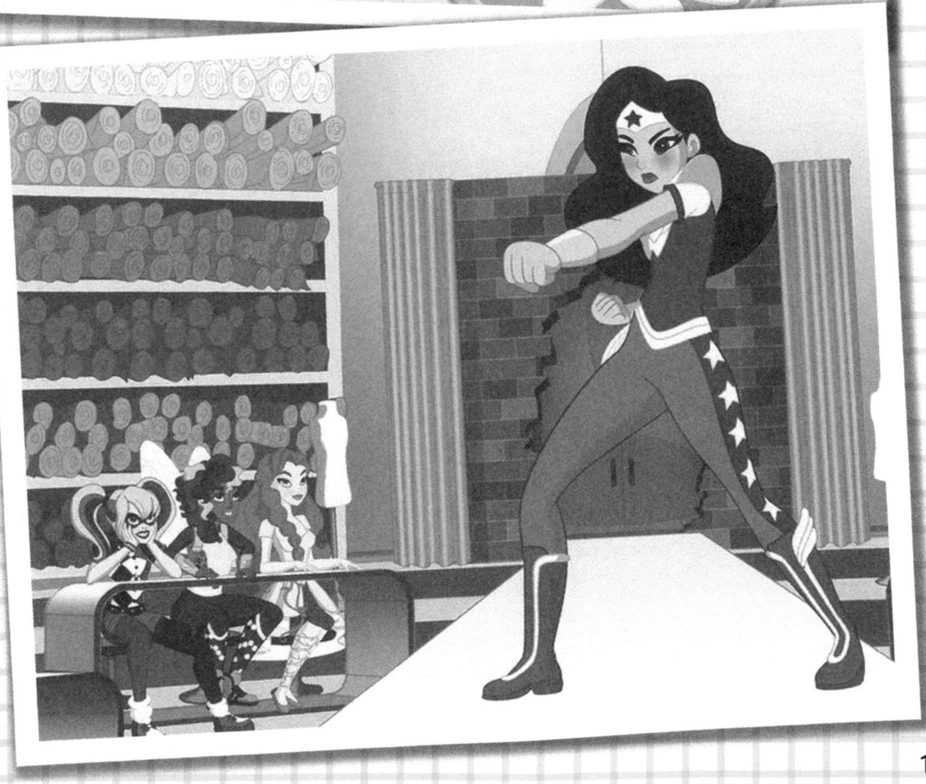

Art and Grace

If you were an expert with a sword, like Katana, what would your sword look like? Be as creative as you like!

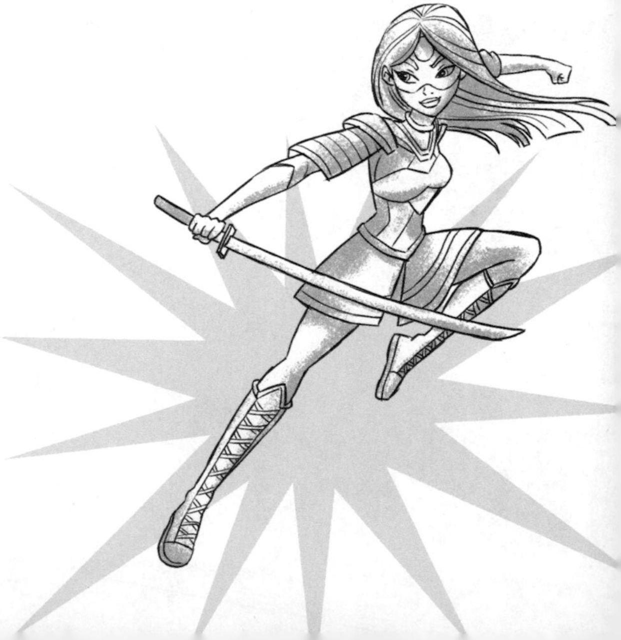

Design a Door Hanger

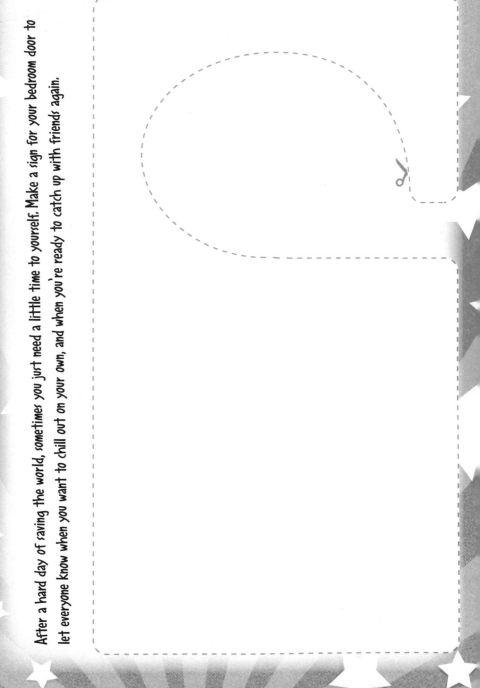

After a hard day of saving the world, sometimes you just need a little time to yourself. Make a sign for your bedroom door to let everyone know when you want to chill out on your own, and when you're ready to catch up with friends again.

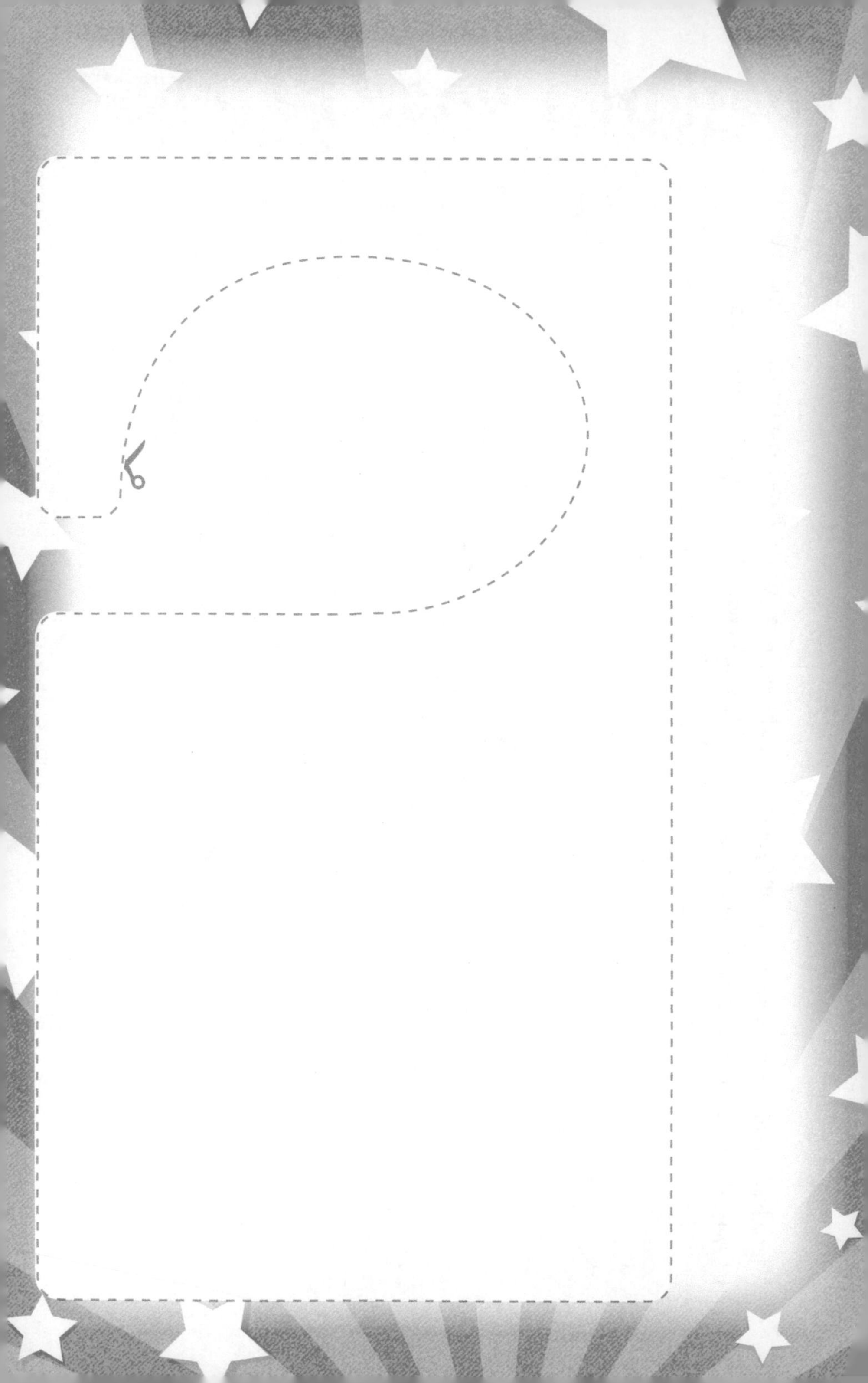

BUZZZZ!

Draw yourself in
a super hero suit
with wings, like
Bumblebee's.

113

SUPER HERO WHEELS

Design your own super hero wheels so you can travel in style everywhere you go.

My Day in a Comic

Draw your day in comic book style! Remember to include speech bubbles and sound effects, too.

Design Disasters

Wonder Woman doesn't like these costume ideas—they're just not her. Try tweaking the designs to make them suit her personality better.

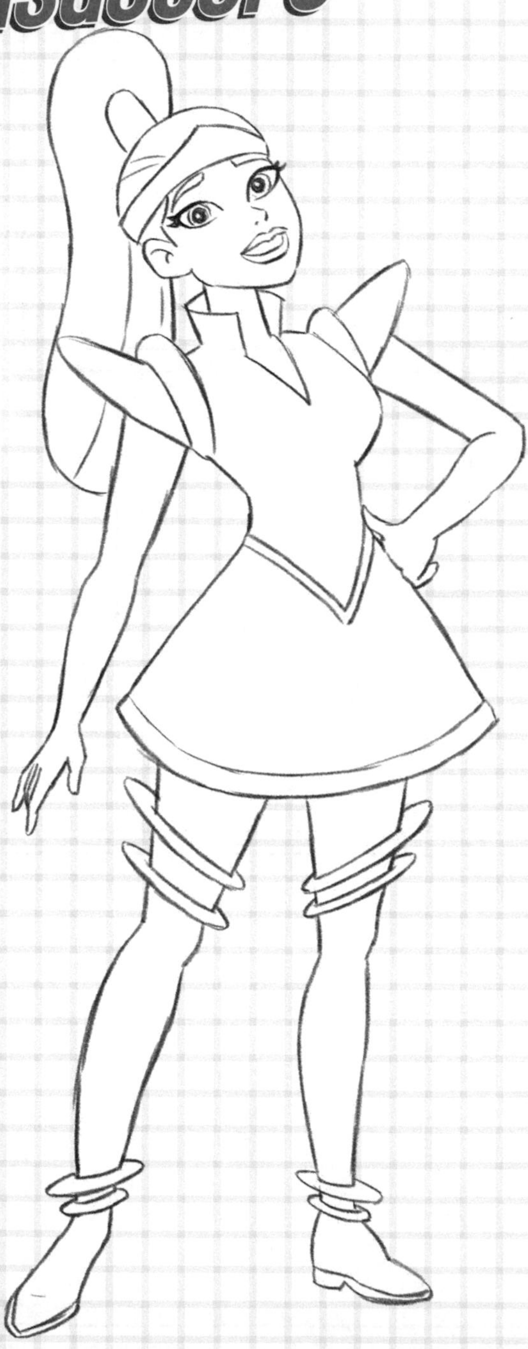

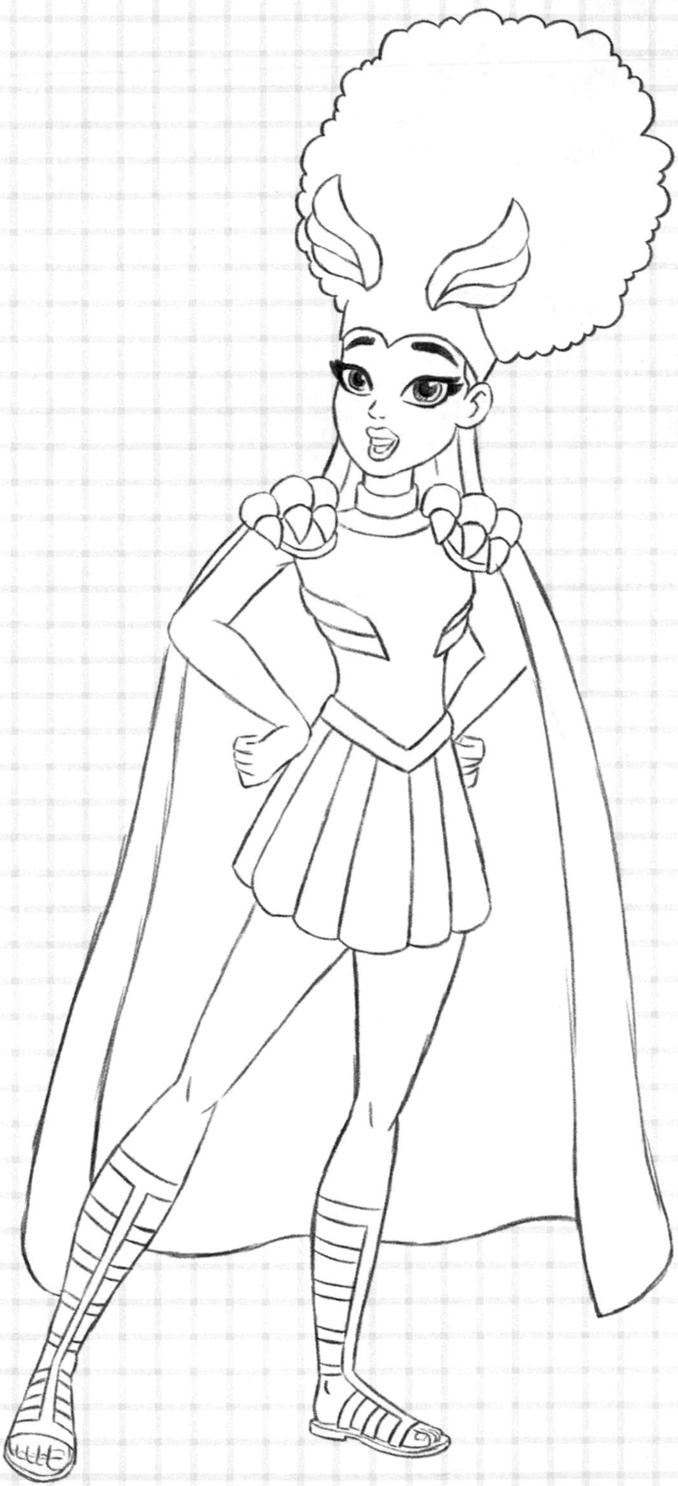

A BEAST OF A DAY

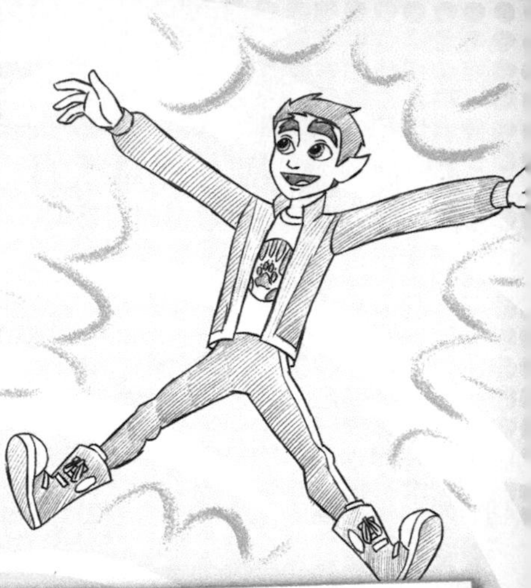

You have Beast Boy's power to change into any animal you choose, just for ONE day. What do you pick?

Draw it here.

Quick Assignment:

QUICK DRAW!

What does Harley Quinn have in her hand? Draw it.

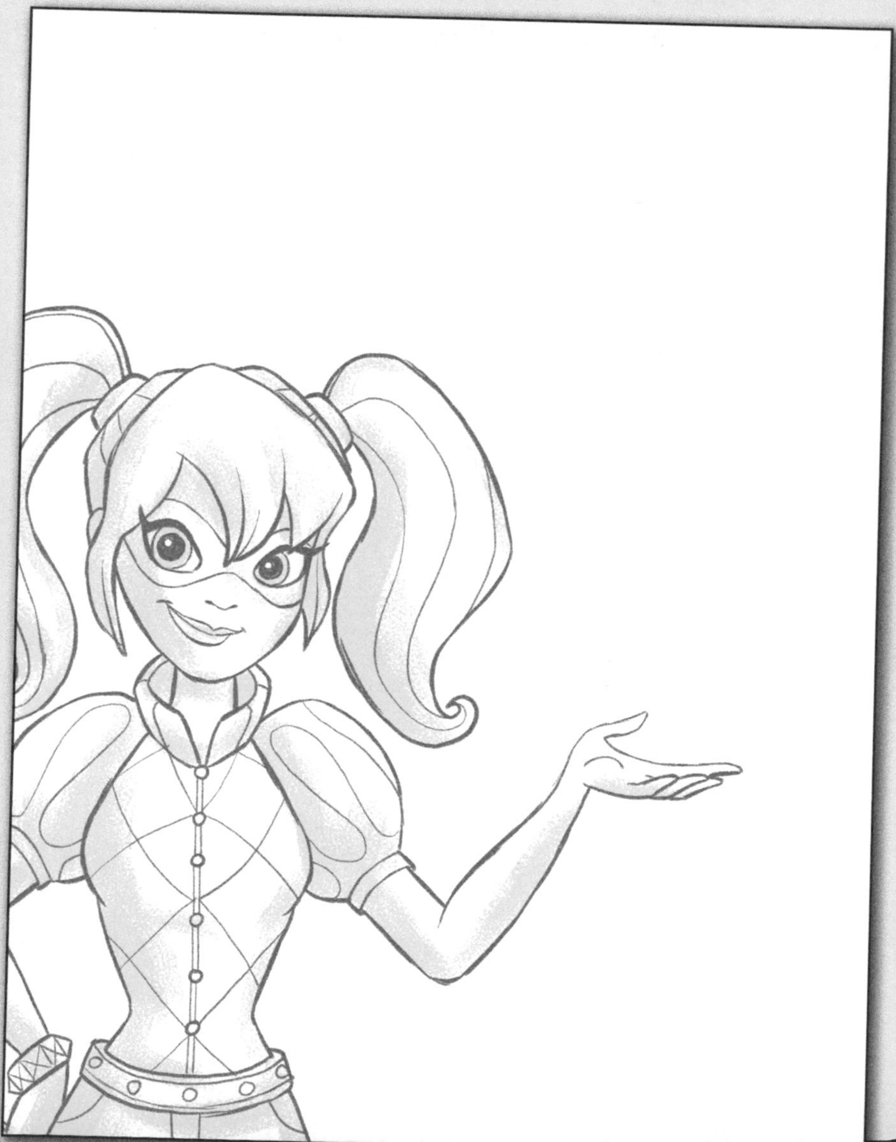

Sleepy Time

Wonder Woman wants superpowered new pajamas!
Design a onesie for her here. Remember,
she may need to jump into action at any
point, so think practically, too.

z z z z z z z z z

Super Hero Fortune-Teller

Follow the steps below to make your own super hero fortune-teller.

1. Cut out the square of paper on the opposite page.
2. Fold along the dotted horizontal and vertical lines, then open the paper again.
3. Fold along the dotted diagonal lines, then open the paper again.
4. Fold the four corners of the square into the middle as shown.

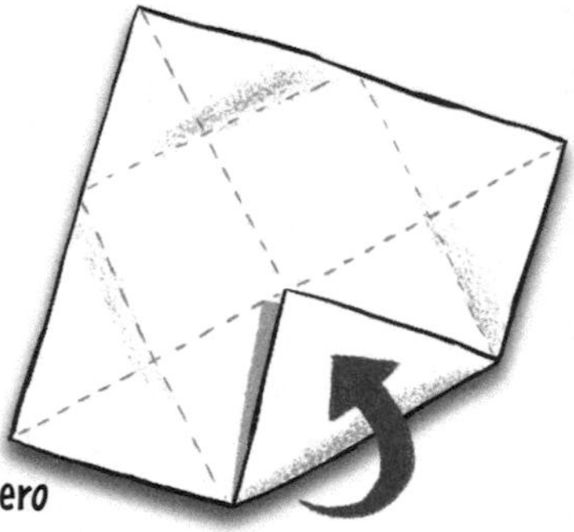

5. Turn the paper over and write one super hero fortune on each of the eight triangle shapes creased into the paper. One has been filled in already.
6. Fold the four corners of the square into the middle as shown.
7. Write a superpower on each one of the eight creased triangles. Four have been filled in already.

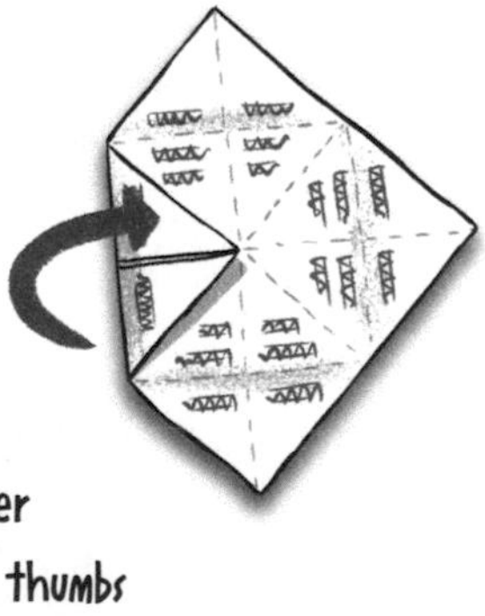

8. Turn the paper over again. Open the paper with your fingers, making room for your thumbs and index fingers to hold and move the fortune-teller.
9. Turn the paper over. You should find the images of the DC Super Hero Girls on the four sections. Your Super Hero Fortune-Teller is ready!

Draw!

SUP

Dr...
s...

How to Play

1. Ask a friend to choose one of the DC Super Hero Girls from the four on top of the fortune-teller.

2. Move your fingers in and out, spelling the super hero's name aloud as you do.

3. Next, ask your friend to choose a superpower. Move your fingers in and out as you spell the power aloud.

4. Finally, ask your friend to choose another superpower. Then lift the flap to see their fortune!

SUPER HERO HIGH

It's your turn to create a display for the bulletin board. What important messages do you want to share with your classmates? What's your theme, and what does the display look like?

SCHOOL BULLETIN BOARD

THE ULTIMATE SUPERPOWER

You have the power to do absolutely anything for a day. What would you do? Write and draw your answer below!

SHHS

Personalize the SHHS logo with your own drawings and doodles.

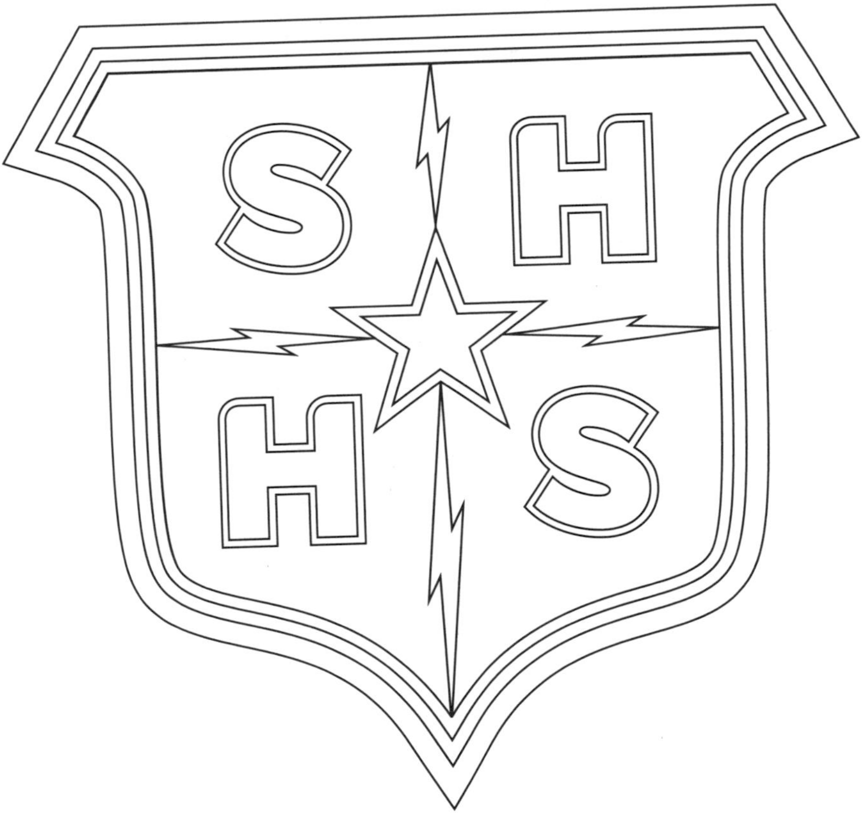
S H
H S

SAVE RAINBOW!

Rainbow the kitten needs rescuing . . . as usual! Which route should Bumblebee take to save the day?

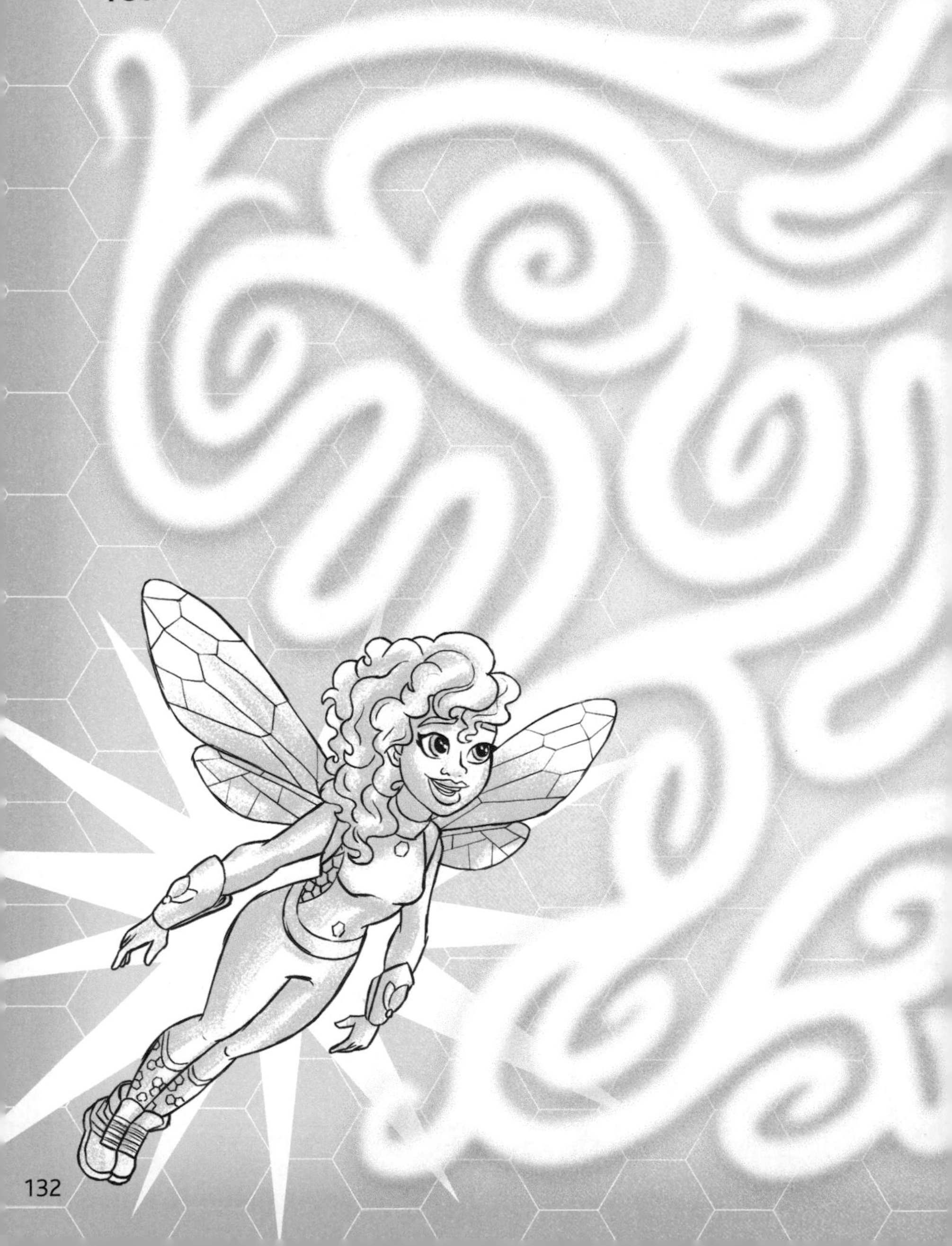

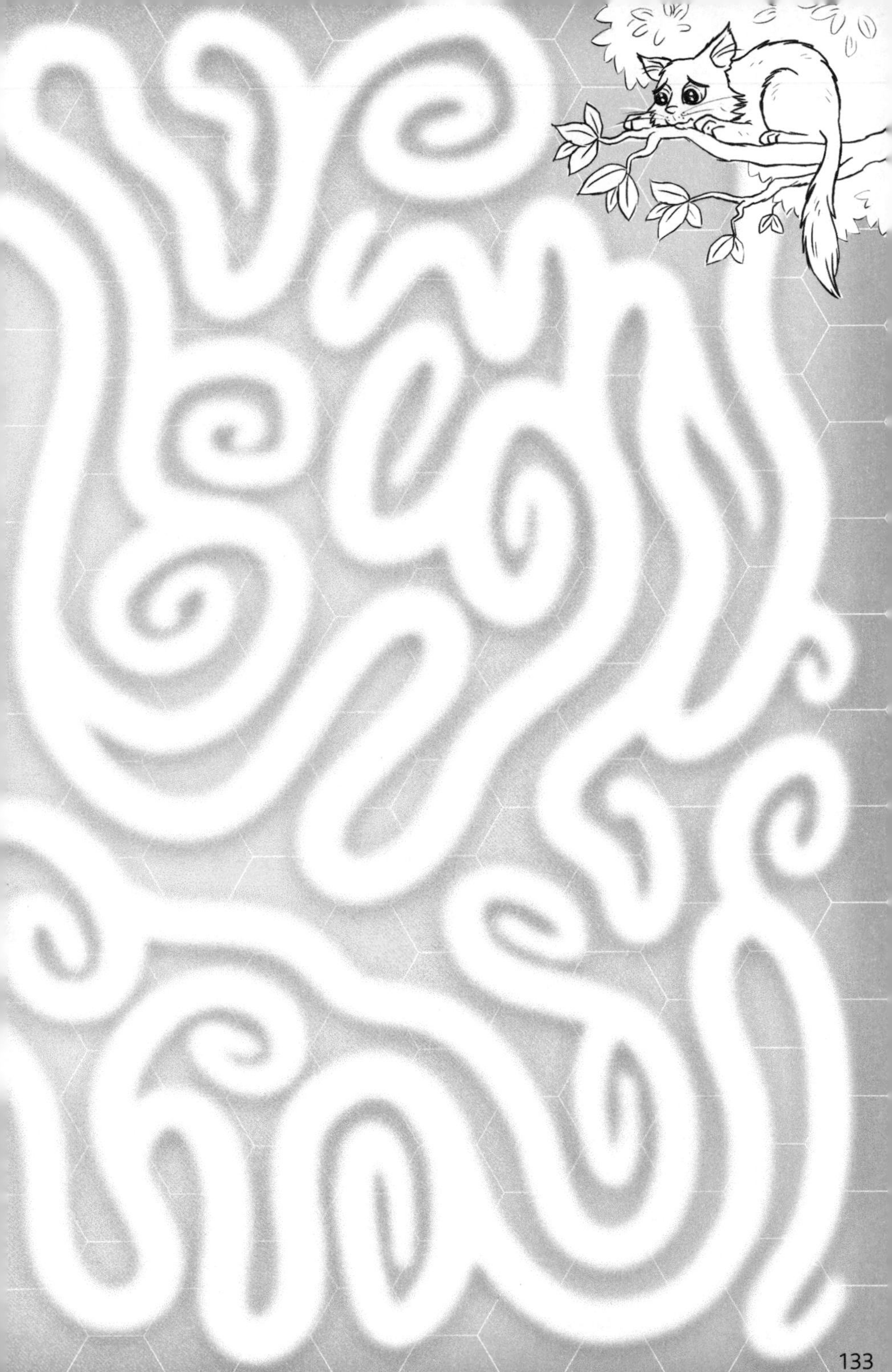

Super Hero Signatures

One day you might become famous for all your good deeds! Practice your signature here for when you're asked to sign autographs for all your fans.

COLOR CODED

Use the color key on the next page to color in these pictures of Hawkgirl and Starfire.

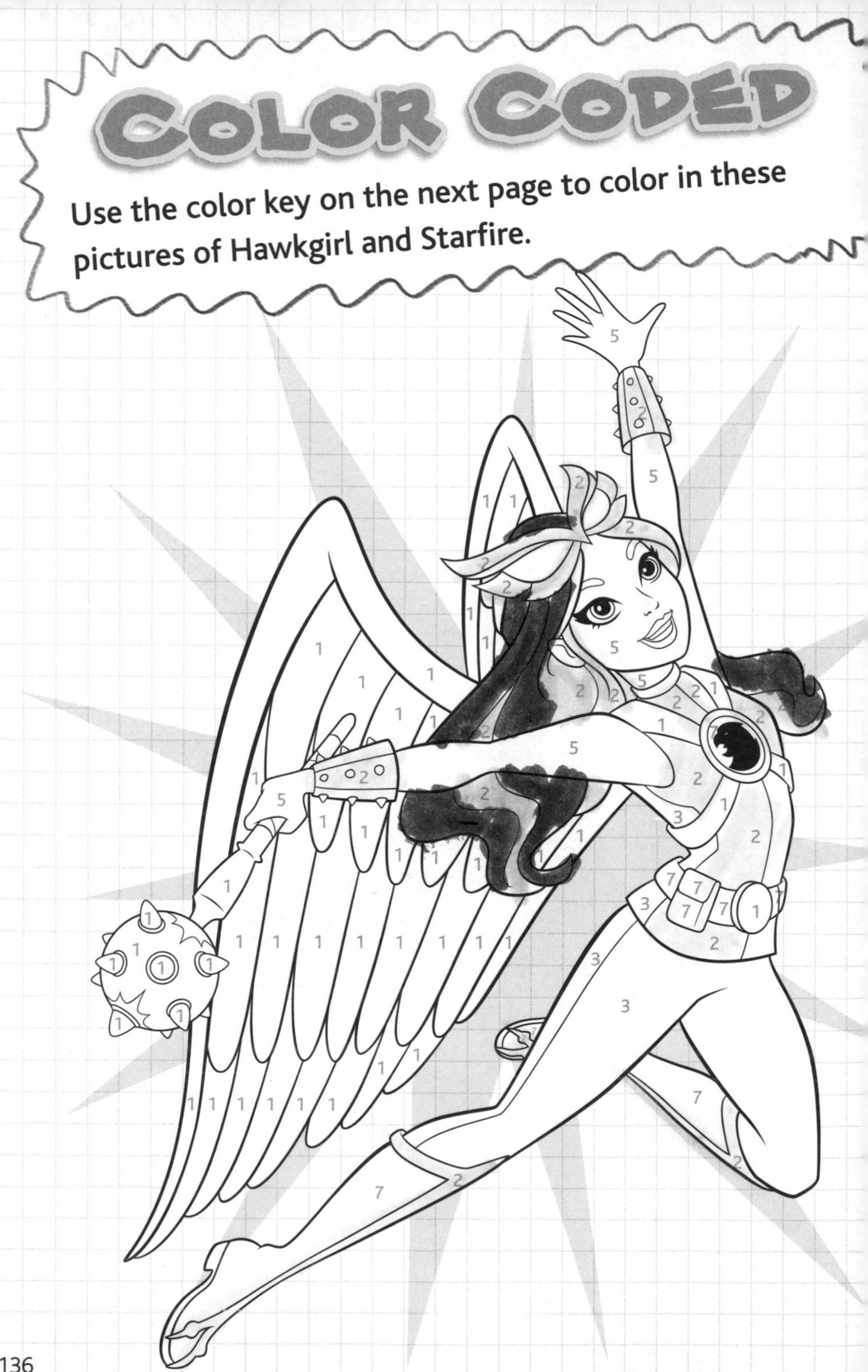

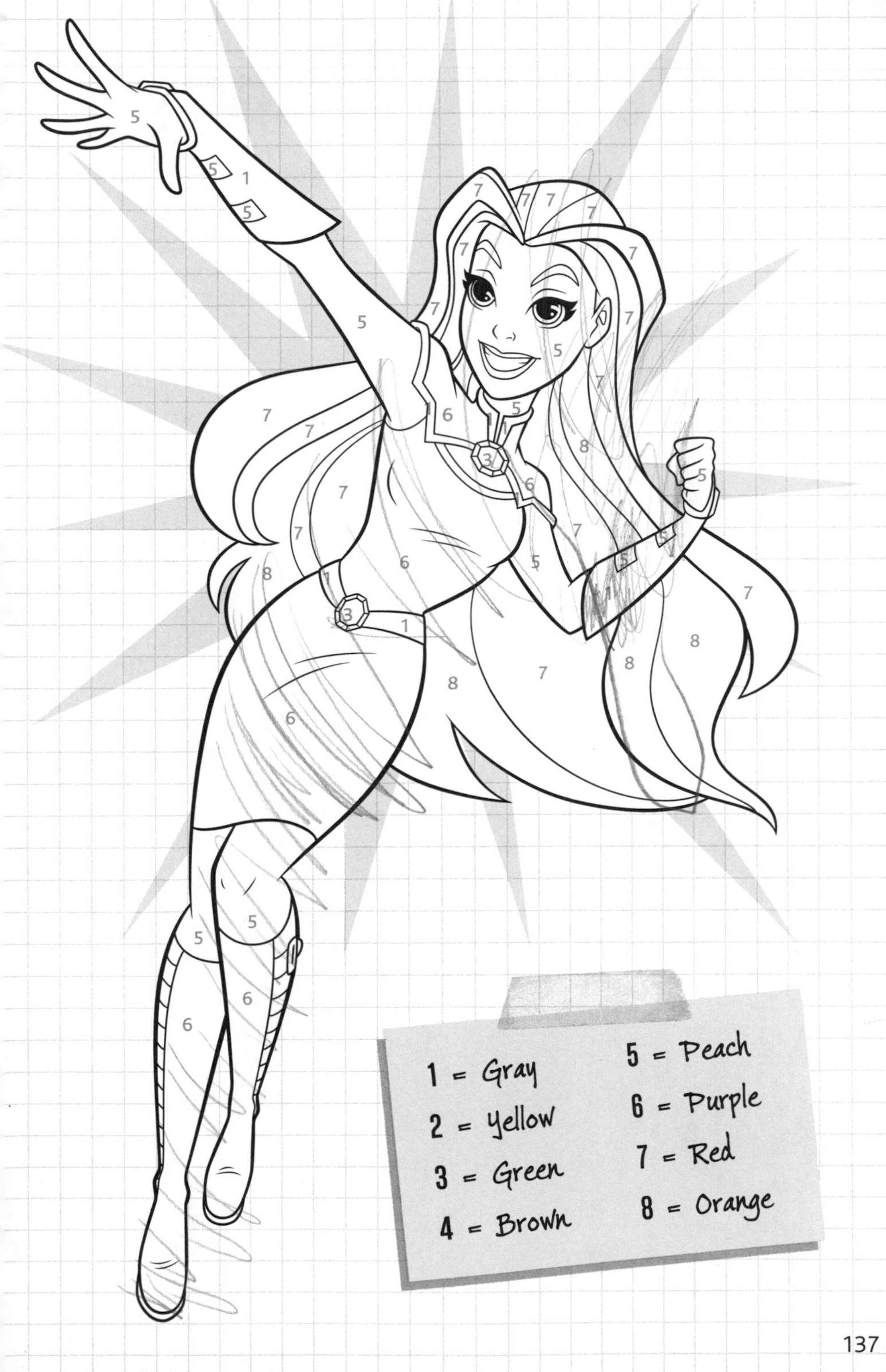

1 = Gray
2 = Yellow
3 = Green
4 = Brown
5 = Peach
6 = Purple
7 = Red
8 = Orange

A Hero's Holiday

Even super heroes need a rest every now and then.
Draw and describe your dream holiday here.

Quick Assignment:

PUZZLED?

Make your own puzzle! Color in the picture. Then cut out the pieces and challenge a friend to put them back together.

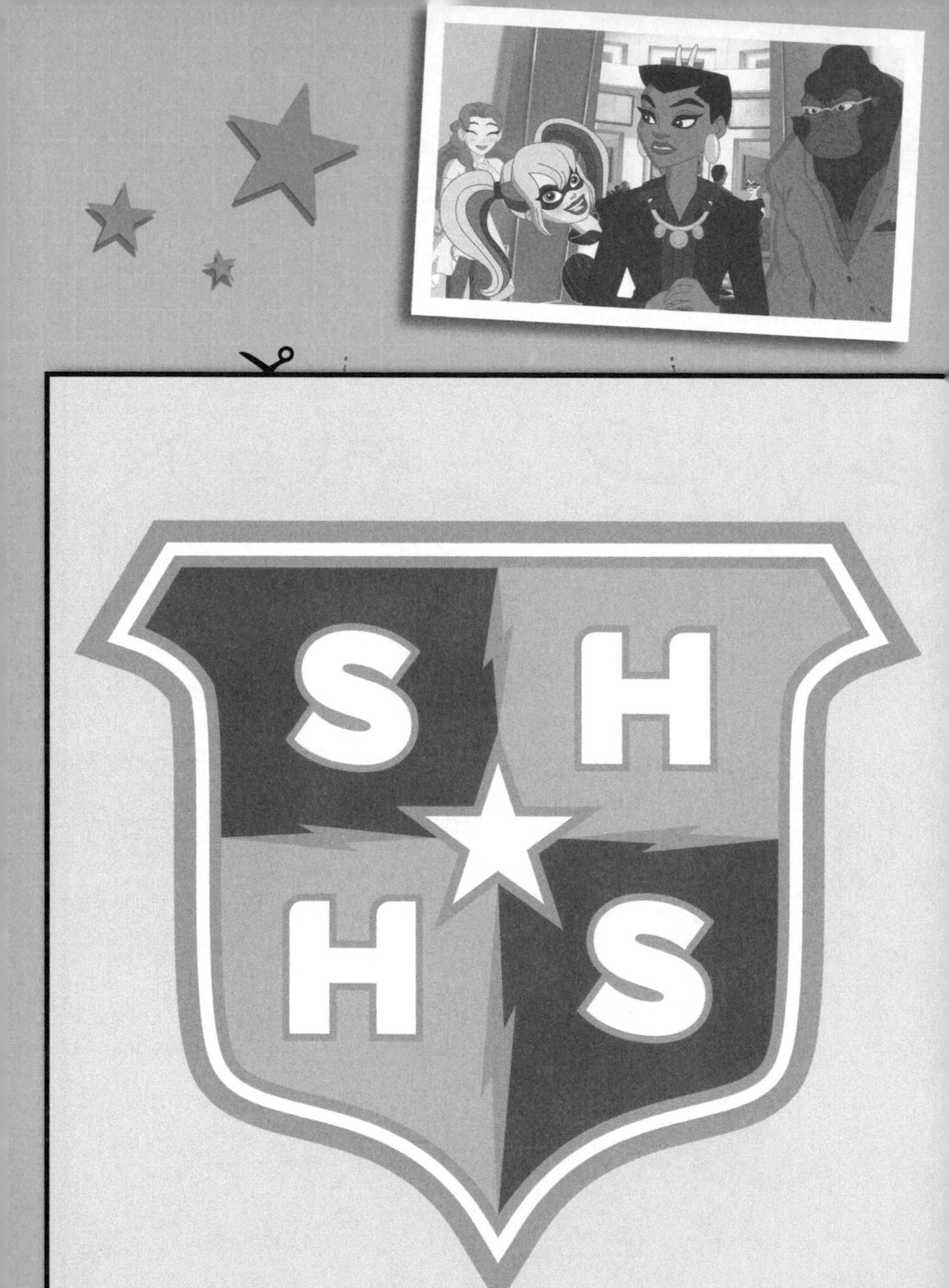

S H
H S

WONDER WOMAN'S LASSO OF TRUTH

Close your eyes and try to circle as many things as you can without taking your pen or pencil off the page.

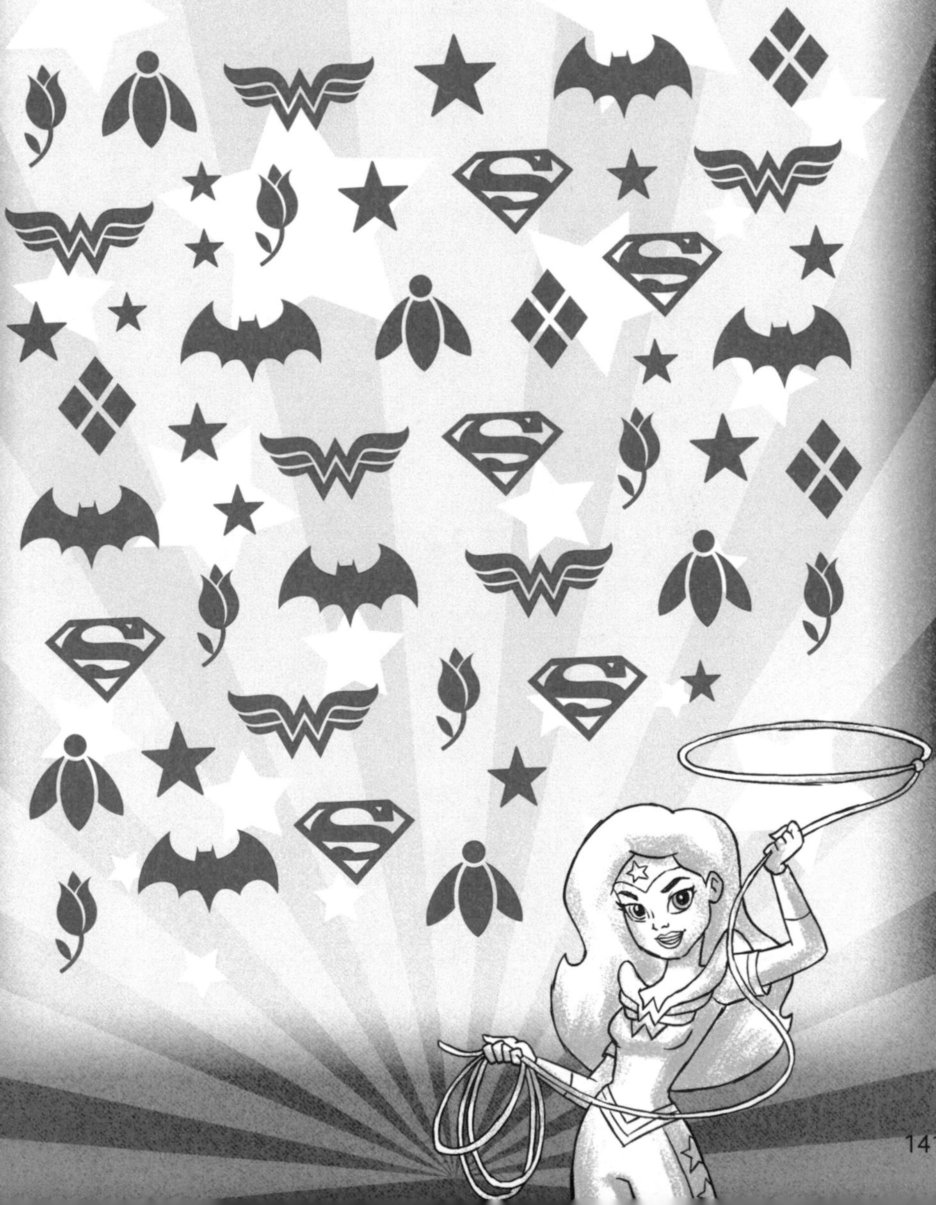

Harley Quinn is putting together a short film all about YOU. You want to make sure you're involved in making it—who knows what she might say otherwise! Describe what happens in your movie or write the script here.

Save the Day Skills

How resourceful are you? Find a way out of these difficult Save the Day situations.

1 Mr. Fox was taking his jet pack for a test run when he crashed into the Amethyst on top of Super Hero High. He's dangling by one hand and the Amethyst looks like it's going to fall! What do you do?

2 A citizen of Metropolis is stuck on top of a burning building, but the fire engine's ladder is too short to reach. No one with the ability to fly is around. What do you do?

3 You've dropped your keys down a drain and you don't have another set. What do you do?

4 A vicious cactus plant has mutated and taken over the whole school. What do you do?

5 You're trying to save the day, but your new super hero suit is holding you back. What do you do?

In the Shadows

Practice your perception skills! Which of the shadows match this picture of Poison Ivy?

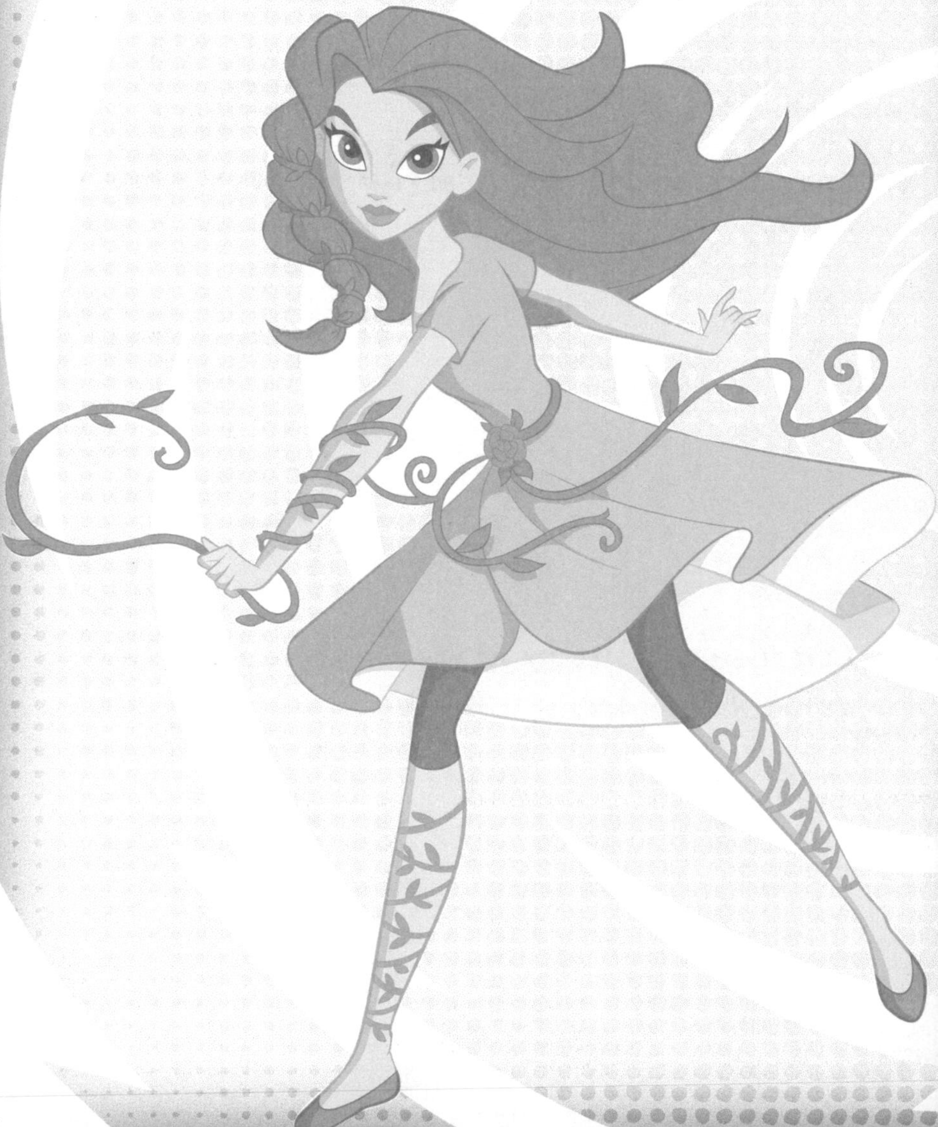

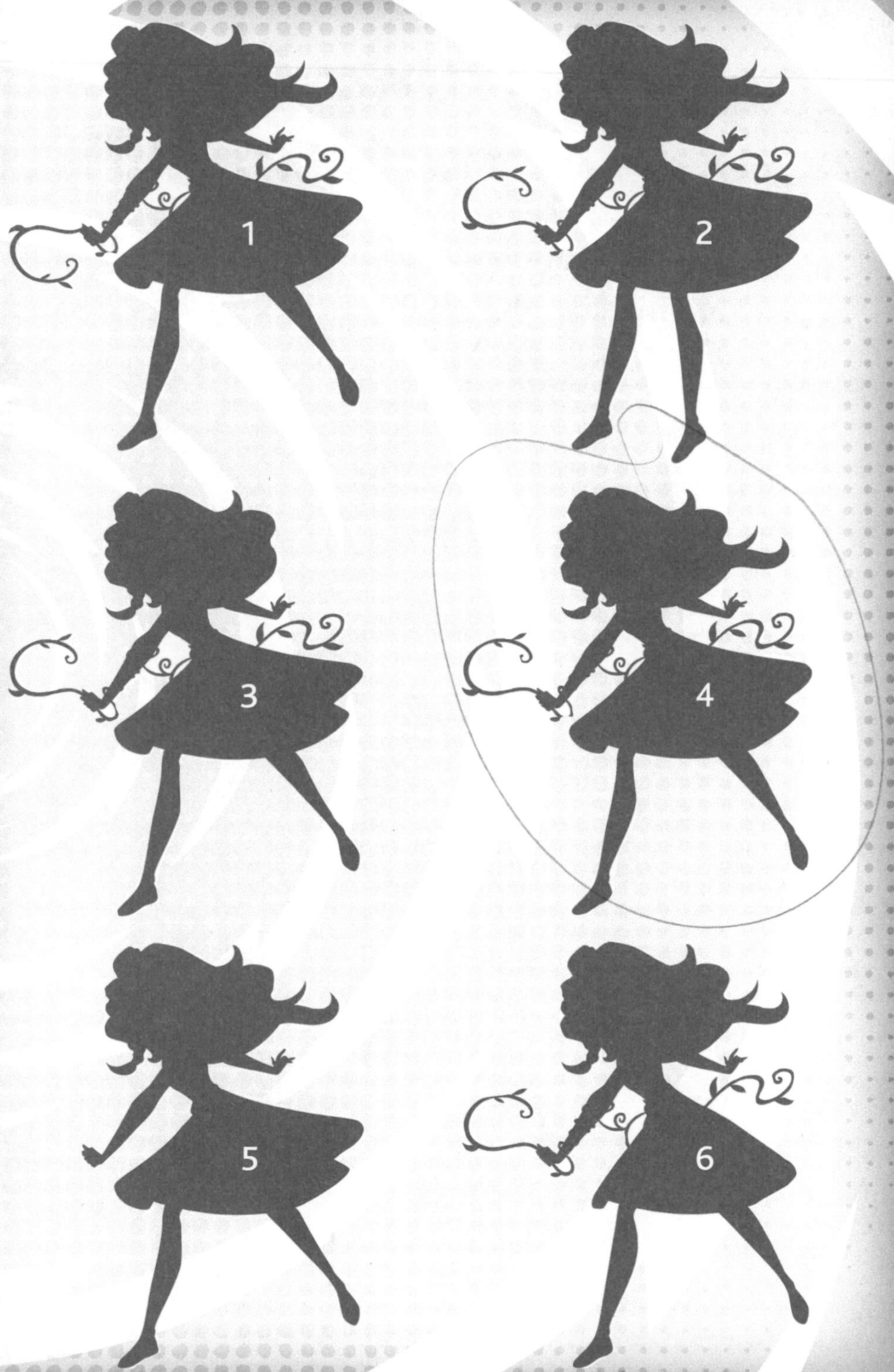
1
2
3
4
5
6

Answer: 4 is the matching shadow.

Draw Your Own Super Hero Snapshot!

It's time for the end-of-year picture of you and your super hero friends—draw it here.

FINAL QUIZ

How well do you know your classmates at Super Hero High? Take a look at the descriptions and guess who each one is.

 I'm kind, optimistic, and super-strong, but I can be a little clumsy at times.

I am _____.

I'm outgoing and full of energy, with the ability to shrink.

I am _____.

I'm intelligent, a great detective, and a techno-wizard.

I am _____.

I'm funky, fearless, and good with a sword.

I am _____.

 I'm catty and charismatic, and I'll do whatever it takes to get my way.

I am _____.

6 I'm shy and prefer the company of plants.

I am ________________________________.

7 I'm an independent and feisty feline who loves wearing black.

I am ________________________________.

8 I'm courageous, competitive, and love taking the lead.

I am ________________________________.

9 I have wings, love planning, and always follow the rules.

I am ________________________________.

10 I'm acrobatic, fun, quick-witted, and completely unpredictable.

I am ________________________________.

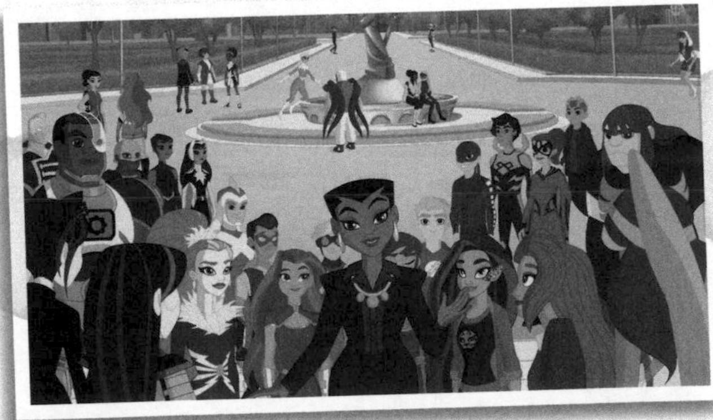

Answers: 1. Supergirl 2. Bumblebee 3. Batgirl 4. Katana 5. Cheetah 6. Poison Ivy 7. Catwoman 8. Wonder Woman 9. Hawkgirl 10. Harley Quinn

What about you? Describe your super self below.

I am
_____

End-of-Year Party Plans

It's up to you to organize a special super hero end-of-year party. Fill in the details and make it the best party yet!

Theme:

Location:

What do the decorations look like?

Playlist:

Entertainment:

Superpowered games:

Prizes:

What's on the food table?

Now draw everyone having fun!

My Superpowered Life

Keep your super hero training notes and record tales of your adventures in the journal pages here.

Who Will You Become?

Record your super hero dreams for the future here.

CONGRATULATIONS!

You saved the day, got an A+, and showed super hero skills along the way!

Fill in your name on this Award Certificate from Super Hero High School.

_____

has successfully completed her first year of super hero training!

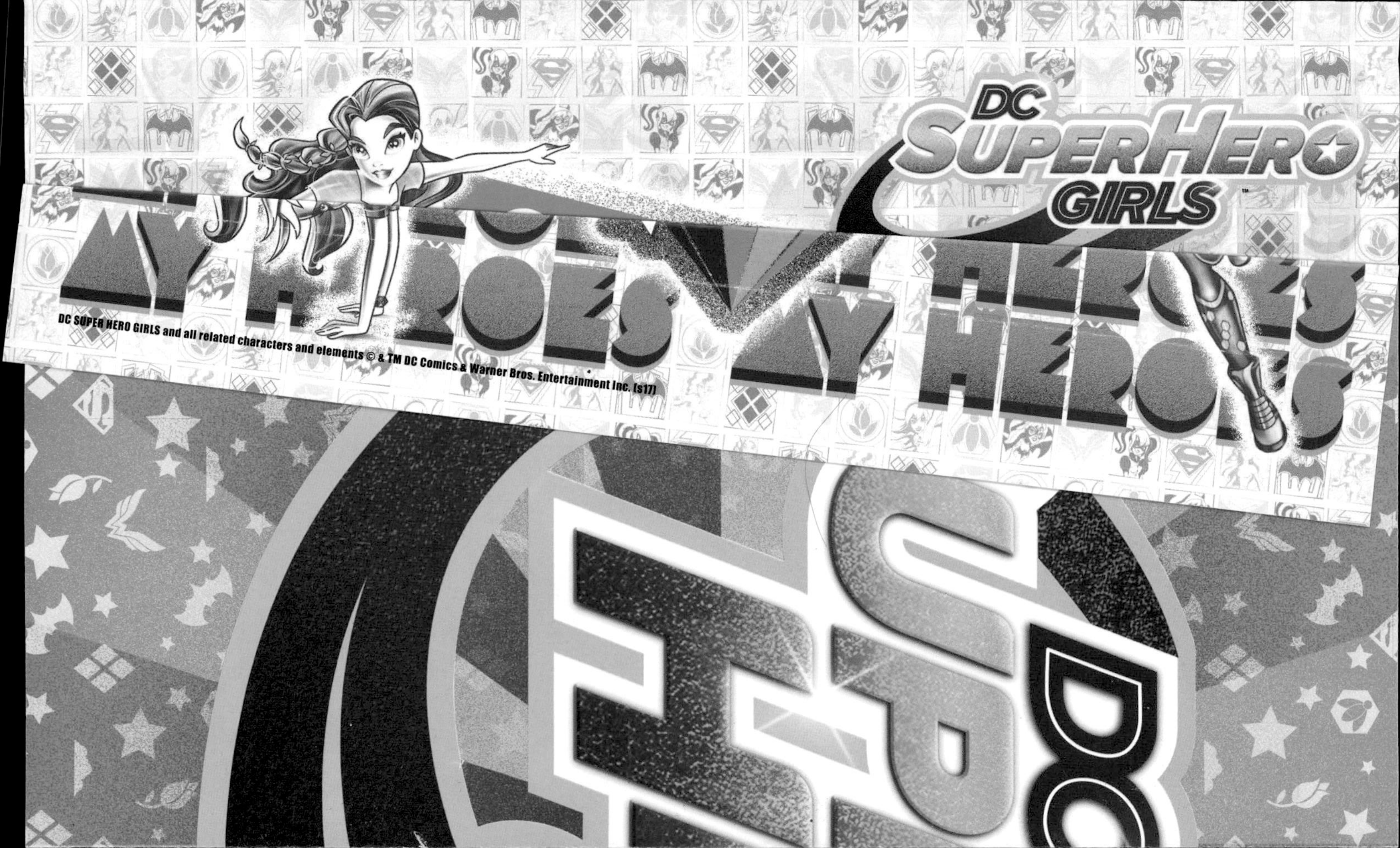
DC SUPERHERO GIRLS™

ER
ERO
GIRLS™

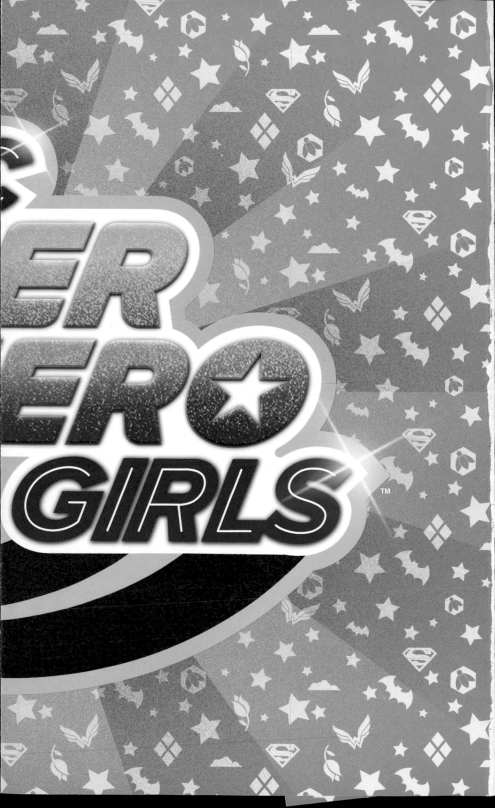